"My financial supp___
has a price."

Something inside her stomach curled into a painful knot. "And that is?"

"A reconciliation." Succinct, blatant and chillingly inflexible.

From somewhere Sandrine dredged up the courage to confront him. "A marriage certificate doesn't transform me into a chattel you own."

Michel's smile bore not the slightest degree of humor. "No discussion, no negotiation. Just a simple *yes* or *no*."

How could he deem something so complicated as *simple?* "You can't demand conditions."

"Watch me."

"Blackmail, Michel?"

HELEN BIANCHIN was born in New Zealand and traveled to Australia before marrying her Italian-born husband. After three years they moved, returned to New Zealand with their daughter, had two sons then resettled in Australia. Encouraged by friends to recount anecdotes of her years as a tobacco sharefarmer's wife living in an Italian community, Helen began setting words on paper, and her first novel was published in 1975. An animal lover, she says her terrier and new Persian kitten regard her study as as much theirs as hers.

USA Today bestselling author **Helen Bianchin** loves to write about the emotional tension between married couples: the passion, the conflict…and the romance! Marriage is the theme of this story—and look out for *The Husband Assignment*, the thrilling sequel to *The Marriage Deal*, on sale in July!

Helen Bianchin

THE MARRIAGE DEAL

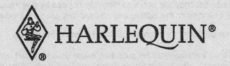

TORONTO • NEW YORK • LONDON
AMSTERDAM • PARIS • SYDNEY • HAMBURG
STOCKHOLM • ATHENS • TOKYO • MILAN • MADRID
PRAGUE • WARSAW • BUDAPEST • AUCKLAND

ISBN 0-373-12097-4

THE MARRIAGE DEAL

First North American Publication 2000.

Copyright © 2000 by Helen Bianchin.

This edition published by arrangement with Harlequin Books S.A.

® and TM are trademarks of the publisher. Trademarks indicated with
® are registered in the United States Patent and Trademark Office, the
Canadian Trade Marks Office and in other countries.

Visit us at www.romance.net

Printed in U.S.A.

CHAPTER ONE

'CUT,' the director called. 'That's a wrap.'

They were the sweetest words she'd heard all day, Sandrine decided as she lifted a hand to ease the weight of her elaborate wig.

Period costume was not the most comfortable wearing apparel, nor was the boned, tightly laced corselet worn to achieve an eighteen-inch waist and push her breasts impossibly high and bare them almost to the point of indecent exposure.

Add the heat of the studio lights, a lead actor who had an inflated ego and delusions of grandeur, the director from hell, and the axiom, 'One should suffer in the name of one's art', had never been more pertinent.

'A word, sweetheart.'

From Tony's lips, *sweetheart* was not a term of endearment, and she froze, then she turned slowly to face the aging director whose talent was legend, but whose manner on occasion belonged in a backstreet of Naples.

'Dinner tonight, my place. Seven.' Hard dark eyes speared hers. 'Be there.' He turned his head and swept an arm to encompass five of her fellow actors. 'Everyone.'

Sandrine stifled a faint groan. All she wanted to do was to change, shower, put on her own clothes and drive to the waterfront villa she called home for the duration of filming, catch a snack and read through her lines for tomorrow.

'Do we get to ask *why*?' the lead actor queried petulantly.

'Money. The film needs it. My guest has it,' the director declared succinctly. 'If his request to meet the cast will clinch an essential injection of funds, so be it.'

'Tonight?' Sandrine reiterated, and suffered the dark lance of his gaze.

'Do you have a problem with that?'

If she did, voicing it would do no good at all, and she affected an eloquent shrug in resignation. 'I guess not.'

He swung an eagle eye over the rest of the cast. 'Anyone else?'

'You could have given us more notice,' the lead actor complained, and earned an earthy oath for his temerity.

'Difficult, when the man only arrived in the country yesterday.'

'Okay, Okay, I get the picture.'

'Pleased to hear it,' was the cryptic response. 'Continuity,' he commanded, and Sandrine gave a heartfelt sigh.

Fifteen minutes later she was done with wardrobe, and she crossed the car park and slid in behind the wheel of her hire-car. Dressed in casual shorts and top, her long sable hair wound into a careless knot atop her head made for comfort in the intense afternoon heat.

Sandrine activated the air-conditioning the instant the engine purred into life, and minutes later she gained the main southern highway.

Her leased accommodation was a two-level villa overlooking water at Sanctuary Cove, a prestigious suburb on Queensland's Gold Coast, only a ten-minute drive from the Coomera film studios.

She activated the CD player as she took the Hope Island-Sanctuary Cove exit ramp and let the funky beat ease the kinks of a rough day.

A tree-lined river wound its way towards a man-made canal system, a nest of beautiful homes and the lush grounds of a popular golf course.

A view that exuded peace and tranquillity, she conceded as she veered towards Sanctuary Cove, then, clear of the security gate guarding the entrance to one of several residential areas, she took the gently curved road leading to the clutch of two-level villas hugging the waterfront.

Cement-rendered brick, painted pale blue with white trim, pebbled gardens adorned with decorative urns provided a pleasant, refreshing facade, Sandrine acknowledged as she used a remote control to open the garage door.

Inside, there was an abundance of cool marble floors, sleek lacquered furniture, soft leather sofas and chairs, and the kitchen was a gourmand's delight with a wealth of modern appliances. The open-plan design was pleasing, encompassing a wide curved staircase at the far end of the foyer leading to a gallery circling the upper floor, where three large bedrooms, each with an en suite, reposed.

Wide, sliding glass doors opened from the lounge and dining room onto a paved terrace that led to a private swimming pool. There was also a boat ramp.

Sandrine discarded her bag, changed into a bikini and spent precious minutes exercising by swimming a few laps of the pool. She needed the physical release, the coolness of the water, in a bid to rid herself of the persistent edge of tension.

A shower did much to restore her energy level, and she towelled her hair, then used a hand-held dryer to complete the process before crossing to the large walk-in robe.

Basic black, she decided as she riffled through her limited wardrobe. A social existence hadn't been uppermost in her mind when she'd hurriedly packed for this particular sojourn, and most of her clothes were divided between three luxurious homes far distant from this temporary residence.

Don't even *think* about those homes or the man she'd shared them with, she determined as she cast a designer gown onto the bed, then extracted stiletto-heeled pumps and an evening bag in matching black.

Yet the image invaded her mind, his broad, sculpted features with their angles and planes hauntingly vivid. Slate-grey eyes seemed to pierce right through to her soul, and she shivered at the memory of his mouth, its sensual curves and the devastating skill of its touch.

Michel Lanier. Mid-thirties, and ten years her senior. Successful entrepreneur, patron of the arts, dark-haired, dark-eyed, with the features of a Renaissance prince and the skilled mentality of a street warrior. Born of French parents in Paris, he'd begun his education in France and completed it in America.

Husband, *lover*. A man who'd swept her into his arms, his heart, and made her his wife.

They'd met at the party of a mutual friend in New York. Sandrine had just completed a modelling assignment during a seasonal break and was due to return to Sydney the following week to resume the filming of a long-running Australian-based television series.

Sandrine flew in with Michel at her side, and within a week she'd introduced him to her family, announced her engagement and had the script writers rewrite her part in the series. As soon as the chilling episodes filming her character's accident and demise were completed, she accompanied Michel back to New York.

Two months later they were married quietly in a very private ceremony among immediate family, and divided their time between New York and Paris. Michel bought a luxury apartment in Sydney's prestigious Double Bay with magnificent views out over the harbour. Their Australian base, he explained.

For six months everything was perfect. Too perfect, Sandrine reflected as she selected black underwear and donned it, then pulled on filmy black hose before crossing to the mirror to begin applying make-up.

The problem had begun three months ago when they spent two weeks in Sydney and a friend gave her a script to read. The story was good, better than good, and she felt an immediate affinity with the supporting character. A vision of how the part should be played filled her head and refused to leave.

Sandrine had known the production time frame wouldn't fit in with Michel's European schedule. She told herself there was no way he'd agree to her spending four weeks in Australia without him.

On a whim she decided to audition, aware her chance of success was next to nil, and she'd almost dismissed it from her mind when, days later, they returned to New York.

Her agent's call confirming she had the part brought a mixture of excitement and trepidation. Production was due to begin in a month at the Coomera studios in Queensland.

She signed the contract when it arrived but delayed telling Michel, all too aware what his reaction would be. Each day that passed had made the telling more difficult, until there were too few days left.

A hundred times she'd rehearsed the words in her mind, yet none of them came out sounding right, and what began as a discussion rapidly digressed into an argument of such magnitude she'd simply thrown some clothes into a bag in the early hours of the morning and booked into a hotel until it was time to take her scheduled flight to Brisbane.

Sandrine had qualified that four weeks wasn't a lifetime, yet with every passing day the physical and spiritual distance between then widened to a point where she feared it might never be repaired.

Worse, Murphy's Law descended, and production had suffered one delay after another. An estimated four weeks extended to five, then six. Budget was shot to pieces as they went into their seventh week. The subtropical midsummer heat was a killer, and tempers frequently ran short as professionalism was pushed to the limit.

Sandrine stood back from the mirror, secured the last pin in the simple knot of hair atop her head, then slid her feet into the elegant black pumps, collected her evening bag and made her way downstairs.

The day's high temperatures had gone down a notch or two, and there was a slight sea breeze teasing the early evening air as Sandrine crossed the paved apron to the entrance of Tony's Main Beach apartment building.

Minutes later she rode the lift to a designated floor and joined the group of fellow thespians enjoying a cool drink on the wide, curved balcony overlooking the ocean.

A portable barbecue had been set up, and a hired chef was organising a selection of seafood, prawns and kebabs ready for grilling.

Sandrine accepted a wine spritzer and sipped it slowly as she cast the guests an idle glance. All present and accounted for, with the exception of the guest of honour, she perceived, and pondered his identity.

'Smile, darling. It's almost "show time" and we're expected to shine,' a husky male voice intoned close to her ear.

She turned slowly to face the lead actor, whose birth

name had been changed by deed poll to Gregor Anders. He was handsome in a rugged, rakish way and took his studio-generated image far too seriously, acquiring so many layers during his professional career it was almost impossible to detect the real man beneath the projected persona.

'Gregor,' Sandrine greeted coolly, and summoned a smile to lessen the sting of her words. 'I'm sure you'll shine sufficiently for both of us.'

It was easy to admire his ability as an actor. Not so easy to condone were the subtle games he played for his own amusement. Yet his name was a drawcard. Women adored his looks, his physique, his sex appeal.

'Now, now, darling,' he chided with a wolfish smile. 'We're supposed to share a rapport, *n'est-ce pas*?' One eyebrow slanted in mocking query.

'On screen, *darling*,' she reminded sweetly, and remained perfectly still as he lifted a hand and traced his forefinger down the length of her arm.

'But it is so much easier to extend the emotions beyond the screen for the duration of filming, don't you agree?'

Her eyes locked with his. 'No.'

'You should loosen up a little,' he cajoled, exerting innate charm.

'I play *before* the camera. Off the set, I suffer no illusions.'

'Strong words,' Gregor murmured. 'I could ensure you regret them.'

'Oh, *please*,' Sandrine protested. 'Go play Mr

Macho with one of the sweet young things who'll simply *swoon* at the thought of receiving your attention.'

'While you've never swooned over a man in your life?'

You're wrong, she almost contradicted, but held her tongue. Gossip ran rife and, in these circles, quickly became embellished until only a grain of recognisable truth remained.

'If you'll excuse me?' She lifted her empty glass a few inches aloft, then turned and crossed to the bar.

Within minutes she was taking a refreshing sip of orange juice. A waiter paused beside her and proffered a tray of hors d'oeuvres. She smiled automatically, selected one, then took a delicate bite. It was delicious and brought an onset of hunger. A sandwich at lunch, followed by an apple and mineral water wasn't much in the way of sustenance.

Sandrine took a mini vol-au-vent and popped it into her mouth.

'Where *is* the guest of honour?' a feminine voice asked in bored tones, and she turned towards the attractive young lead actress.

'Bent on making a grand entrance, perhaps?'

'That's a woman's prerogative, sweetheart.'

The smile was a little too artificial, the voice a fraction too contrived. Cait London had acquired *star* status and wasn't about to let anyone forget it. Especially a fellow actress playing a minor part, Sandrine decided silently.

'No one seems to know who he is,' Cait mused. 'A successful entrepreneur is all Tony will reveal.' An acquisitive gleam darkened her beautiful blue eyes. 'Obviously rich. As long as he's presentable and under sixty, it could prove to be an interesting encounter.'

'And single?' Sandrine posed, only to hear the other's musical laugh.

'*Darling*, who cares?'

Not Cait, obviously.

Minutes later Sandrine detected a change in the buzz of conversation, a shift in tone definition that caused her to lift her head.

So he had finally arrived. Almost a half-hour late.

Some sixth sense alerted her attention, followed by a quick stab of apprehension.

'*Mine*,' Cait uttered, sotto voce.

Even as Sandrine turned slowly to conduct a sweeping appraisal of the room, a telltale prickle of awareness slithered down the length of her spine.

There was only one man who could generate this effect. One man whose soul was so closely attuned to her own they were almost twin halves of a whole.

Sandrine caught sight of a tall male frame, felt the familiar tug on her senses as she recognised the broad-boned, chiselled profile, the dark, conventionally groomed hair, which seven weeks ago had lain longer at his nape, adding a refined, untamed quality that was equally as dangerous as the man himself.

She'd adored threading her fingers through the silky thickness, the purchase it lent when she held fast his head and simply clung during the slow, exquisite torture of his lovemaking, the dazzling heat of their passion.

Those had been the wild, sweet days when there had been only love to guide them, she reflected. A time when she'd given him everything without thought of denial.

Now she watched Michel while he paused in conversation to lift his head as if he, too, sensed her presence. Dark grey eyes locked with hers, probing, intense, and totally lacking in any humour or warmth.

Time stood still as everything and everyone in the room faded to the periphery of her vision.

There was only Michel. The man, the moment, the exigent chemistry evident. She could sense it, *feel* its powerful pull as she became caught up in the magical spell of something so intensely primitive she felt raw, exposed and acutely vulnerable.

Then he smiled, and for an instant she was transported back to the time they first met. Almost a duplicate situation to this, where they'd caught sight of each other at the same time across a crowded room.

Except the past had little place in the present. She could see it in the sudden flare in those beautiful slate-grey eyes and sense it in his stance.

Body language. She'd studied it as part of her craft and she could successfully determine each movement, every gesture.

Did anyone else recognise the cool ruthlessness or define the latent anger that lurked beneath the surface of his control? They lent his features a dark, brooding quality and gave hint to a refined savagery, which unleashed could prove lethal.

He was a man who held no illusions and whose

youthful passage had moulded him, shaping a destiny many of his peers could only envy.

Sandrine watched in mesmerised fascination as he murmured an excuse to their host, then crossed the room and stepped out onto the terrace.

Fine Armani tailoring sheathed an awesome muscle definition in that powerful frame, and every movement held the lithe, flowing grace of a superb jungle animal.

Her heart thudded and quickened to a faster beat. Each separate nerve end became highly sensitised as he moved towards her, and she couldn't think of one sensible word to say in greeting. Considering the carelessly flung words they'd hurled at each other all those weeks ago, a simple hello seemed incredibly banal.

She didn't get the chance, for he captured her shoulders, slid one hand to hold fast her head, then his mouth took possession of hers in a kiss that sent her emotions spinning out of control.

It was claim-staking, she acknowledged dimly when she was able to breathe. Flagrant, seductive and hungry.

Worse was her own reaction as, after the initial shock, she relinquished a hold on sanity and opened her mouth to him.

She savoured the taste and feel of his tongue as it created a swirling, possessive dance with hers and lured her into an emotional vortex where time and place had no meaning.

When he lifted his head, she couldn't move. Gradually she became aware of the sound of background music, the indistinct buzz of conversation, as the room and its occupants filtered into her vision.

Dear heaven. How long had they remained locked in that passionate embrace? Thirty seconds, sixty? More?

All he had to do was touch her and she went up in flames. In seven weeks the passionate intensity hadn't lessened.

What did you expect? a tiny voice taunted. He's haunted your dreams every night since you left him and invaded your thought processes almost to the detriment of your work.

The emotional intensity shimmered between them, exigent, electric and mesmeric. Yet there was also anger, not forgotten nor forgiven.

'What are you doing here?'

Was that her voice? It sounded so cool, so calm, when inside she was a seething mass of conflicting tensions.

'I concluded my business in Europe.'

Important meetings where his presence was paramount. No opportunity for delegation there, she reasoned. What excuse had he given explaining her absence to family in Paris? To his elder brother Raoul, his *grand-mère*?

She experienced a moment's regret and banked down the edge of remorse she felt for the elderly matriarch who ruled with a fist of iron, yet had the heart of a pussycat and of whom she'd become very fond.

'And discovered I wasn't waiting in the New York apartment,' Sandrine voiced evenly. Her chin lifted fractionally and the topaz flecks in her eyes shone deep gold. 'Subdued and contrite at having thwarted you?'

'Difficult,' he acknowledged with wry cynicism. 'When a delayed filming schedule kept you here.'

Sandrine opened her mouth to refute that was something he couldn't have known, then she closed it again. All he had to do was lift the phone and instruct someone to report her every move. It angered her unbearably that he had.

'What's your purpose, Michel?' she launched with polite heat. If they were alone, she would have hit him. Or made every effort to try.

'You didn't answer any of the several messages I left on your message bank.'

She'd let every call go to voice mail and become selective in whose messages she returned. 'What was the point when we'd said it all?'

'Nothing is resolved in anger.'

So he'd let her go, sure in the knowledge that, given time, she'd come to her senses and run back to him? How many nights had she lain awake fighting against the need to do just that? Except pride and determined resolve had kept her firmly where she was. As well as loyalty to a project and a legally binding contract.

She looked at him carefully, noting the fine lines that fanned from the outer corners of his eyes, the faint shadows beneath. Unless it was her imagination, the faint vertical crease slashing each cheek seemed deeper.

Once, those dark grey eyes had gleamed with naked

passion...for her. Only her. She'd looked into their depths and melted.

Now there was only darkness and a hard quality that chilled her bones.

'You haven't explained why you're an invited guest in Tony's apartment,' Sandrine managed evenly, and saw one eyebrow arch.

'You mean you haven't guessed?'

There was soft mockery evident in his tone, an underlying hint of steel that tore the breath from her throat.

'Your sojourn in Europe is over and you've come to haul me home?'

Her facetiousness didn't escape him, and his mouth assumed a cynical slant. 'Try again.'

Anger overlaid fear. 'You want a divorce.'

His expression didn't change, but something in his eyes shifted, hardened. 'There hasn't been a divorce in the Lanier family for three hundred years.'

'You mean women have suffered the overbearing, arrogant, autocratic will of Lanier men for *centuries* without offering a word in complaint?'

'I imagine any complaints were soon—' he paused, the emphasis significant '—satisfactorily dealt with.'

She took his meaning and rode with it. 'Sex isn't the answer to everything.'

'Lovemaking.'

There was a difference. Dear heaven, such a difference. Even *thinking* about Michel's powerful body joining with hers brought a surge of warmth that raced through her veins, heating her body to fever pitch.

He saw the reaction in the subtle shading of her skin, the faint convulsive movement of her throat, the sudden, too rapid sweep of eyelashes as she sought to veil her response. And he experienced satisfaction.

'You haven't answered my question.'

'Which particular question is that?'

Her lashes flew wide, and the intensity of those deep brown, gold-flecked eyes held a brilliance that danced close to anger.

'What you're doing here, *tonight*?'

His gaze was direct, probing, and held a degree of cynical humour. 'Why, *chérie*, I am the guest of honour at this soirée.'

'The guest of honour touted to inject sufficient funds to rescue the film?'

Michel confirmed it with the faint inclination of his head. 'For a price,' he conceded with chilling softness.

Something inside her stomach curled into a painful knot. 'And that is?'

'A reconciliation.' Succinct, blatant and chillingly inflexible.

Dear God. Pious salutation had nothing to do with the words that remained locked in her throat.

From somewhere she dredged up the courage to confront him. 'A marriage certificate doesn't transform me into a chattel you own.'

Michel took in her pale features, the dark eyes that seemed too large for her face, the loss of a few essential kilos, and barely restrained himself from wringing her slender neck.

Sandrine became aware of the circumspect glances,

the ripple of curiosity Michel's action had generated. Cait London's expression was composed, although her brilliant blue eyes were icy.

Their marriage hadn't been written up in any of the international society pages. It was doubtful anyone in this room knew the guest of honour's identity, much less his connection with a little-known supporting actress.

'This is hardly the time or place.'

Michel's smile was a mere facsimile and bore not the slightest degree of humour. 'No discussion, no negotiation. Just a simple yes or no.'

Simple? How could he deem something so complicated as *simple*? 'You can't demand conditions.'

'Watch me.'

'Blackmail, Michel?'

He gave an imperceptible shrug. 'Label it what you will.'

'And if I refuse?' Sandrine queried bravely.

Something moved in those dark eyes, making them appear incredibly dangerous. 'I walk out of here.'

And out of her life? As she'd walked out of his? Temporarily, she amended.

So why did she have the feeling she was poised on the edge of a precipice? One false move and she'd fall to unknown depths?

She could see the grim purpose etched in his features and she felt her stomach muscles clench in pain. 'You don't play fair.'

His expression didn't change. 'This isn't a game.'

No, it wasn't. Yet she hated him for employing manipulative tactics.

'Yes or no,' Michel reiterated with deadly quietness.

CHAPTER TWO

SANDRINE looked at Michel carefully, her eyes steady, her composure seemingly intact. Only she knew what effort it cost to present such a calm facade.

'I'm sure Tony has other sources available from which to raise the necessary money.'

'He has exhausted all of them.'

'How can you know that?' It didn't warrant an answer, she acknowledged wryly. The Lanier family consortium held immense holdings, and Michel was extremely wealthy in his own right. As such, he had contacts and access to otherwise privileged information.

Without the injection of funds, the film wouldn't be completed or make it into the cinemas, and the resulting financial loss would be disastrous.

The knowledge she held the film's fate in her hands didn't sit well. Nor did the fact that Michel had very skilfully planned it this way.

'With the possible exception of Gregor Anders, the film doesn't have the big-name leads to attract a runaway box office success,' Michel relayed with damning accuracy. 'The director and producer are both scrambling to resurrect their ailing careers with a period piece currently out of vogue.'

Add to that, she knew the film's financial backers

had set a limited budget that made little allowance for countless takes in a quest for perfection, delays, escalating expenses, and the result was a high-risk venture no sensible investor would touch.

Sandrine cast him a level look. 'That's your opinion.'

Michel's gaze remained steady, obdurate. 'Not only mine.'

'If that's true, why are you prepared to invest?'

His expression didn't change, and for several seconds she didn't think he was going to answer. 'Honesty, Sandrine?' he mocked lightly. 'You.'

Her eyes widened, then narrowed slightly.

'What did you think I would do, ultimately?' Michel demanded silkily. 'Just let you *walk*?'

She gritted her teeth, counted to five. 'I didn't *walk*,' she denied vehemently. 'I was committed to a signed contract. If I hadn't checked into the studio on the designated date, I could have been sued.'

'A contract you chose not to tell me you'd signed.'

'*You* were locked into meetings in Europe.'

'Aren't you going to introduce me, darling?'

Damn. Sandrine barely swallowed the vengeful curse as Cait placed an arm along the back of her waist in a gesture that indicated they were the closest of friends.

'Michel Lanier,' Michel interposed smoothly.

'Cait London.' The smile, the voice, the actions, combined to provide maximum impact. 'So, you're our knight in shining armour.'

Sandrine watched an exquisitely lacquered nail trace

a provocative pattern down his suit sleeve and was overwhelmed by the desire to sweep it aside.

'And Sandrine's husband.'

Ouch. She felt Cait's slight intake of breath, glimpsed the coy smile and felt the faint increase of pressure as fingers bit into the back of her waist.

'Well,' Cait acknowledged as she turned to shoot Sandrine an icy glare, 'aren't you the secretive one.'

Michel took hold of Sandrine's hand and lifted it to his lips, then he spared Cait a level glance.

'If you'll excuse us? We were in the middle of a private discussion.'

Oh, my. He didn't pull any punches. She watched as the lead actress proffered a sizzling smile, then turned and walked away with a blatant sway of her hips.

'Another conquest,' Sandrine commented lightly.

'Let's focus on the immediate issue, shall we?' The master manipulator. Dammit, why did she want to crack his cool facade when she knew what lay beneath the surface of his control?

His skill with words in the midst of her volatile diatribe had been chilling. Hell, he hadn't even raised his voice. *She* had been the one who'd lost it.

Now he was using that skill to employ invidious blackmail, cleverly positioning her between a rock and a hard place. She was the price, the film her prize.

'You leave me little choice,' she said with deliberate coolness, then waited a beat and added, 'For now.'

He reached out and brushed the back of his fingers down her cheek. 'No conditions.'

She felt her body's betraying response to his touch, the heated sensation that invaded her bones and melted them to molten wax.

Sandrine's eyes deepened, and her mouth shook a little. With anger, resentment and a need to swing into verbal attack mode. Except this wasn't the time or place if she wanted to retain any sense of dignity.

As it was, speculation undoubtedly ran rife among the cast members and fellow guests. Did Tony know that Sandrine Arnette was Michel Lanier's *wife*?

Michel watched as she fought to keep her conflicting emotions under wraps, and defined each and every one of them. With a degree of dispassionate anticipation, he was aware the fight between them had scarcely begun. He intended to win.

'I need a drink,' she admitted, watching as Michel's lips curved to form a musing smile.

He lifted a hand, and in an instant a waitress appeared at his side. Michel had that effect on women. All women, of any age. It was an inherent charm, one he used quite ruthlessly on occasion.

He lifted two flutes of champagne from the tray and handed one to Sandrine.

'*Salut.*' He touched the rim of her flute with his own.

She ignored the temptation to drain the contents in one long swallow and deliberately sipped the chilled aerated wine, savoured the taste, then let the liquid slide down her throat.

'Shall we join our host?'

Sandrine's eyes clashed momentarily with his, then

she veiled their expression. There would be an opportunity later to unleash the verbal diatribe seething beneath the surface. Round one might be his, but she had every intention the next would be hers.

She summoned a slow smile, her acting ability prominent as she tucked a hand into the curve of his elbow.

'Having provided the guests with an unexpected floor show, don't you think introductions are somewhat overdue?'

Minutes later Michel moved easily at Tony's side, displaying an interest in each guest's professional background as he posed questions with practised charm.

Working the room, Sandrine recognized with cynicism. A retentive and photographic memory ensured he was never at a loss in the business arena or among the social set.

'As secrets go, yours is a doozey.'

She turned slightly and encountered a slender young woman whose name temporarily escaped her.

'Stephanie Sommers, marketing.'

'Yes, of course,' Sandrine responded, warming to Stephanie's faintly wicked smile.

'I can understand you keeping him under wraps. Where did you find him?'

'New York. We married in Paris.'

'Ah, the universal city for lovers.'

Sandrine felt a shiver slither its way over the surface of her skin as she experienced instant recall of the city, the ambience. The magic. Paris in the spring, when the grey skies cleared and everything came alive. As her heart had when she first met Michel.

An ache centred in the region of her diaphragm, intensifying as memories surfaced. Memories that had held such promise, so much love, she'd imagined their lives together were inviolate and forever entwined.

The stuff of which fantasies are made, she reflected wryly. With little basis in reality.

'Tony is on his best behaviour.'

Sandrine summoned a quick smile. Something that was becoming a habit as the evening progressed. 'The future of the film is at stake.'

'Is it?'

The query bore a certain quizzical humour as if Stephanie had already concluded the injection of essential finance was a done deal.

It was, although Sandrine wondered what the marketing manager's reaction would be if she discovered the reason for Michel's investment.

'Okay. So the rest of us get to sweat it out a little longer.'

Sandrine looked suitably enigmatic until Stephanie gave a low, throaty chuckle.

'You can't say I didn't try.' The attractive blonde spared a glance at her watch. 'I'm going to have to leave soon.'

'A date?'

'With a baby-sitter who can only stay until ten,' the marketing manager replied with a touch of cynicism.

'Divided loyalties?'

'No contest. My daughter wins out every time.' She

quickly scanned the room, then lowered her voice to a confidential tone. 'Your husband has escaped from Tony and is heading this way. Impressive beast, isn't he?'

Beast was an apt description. Although not in the context Stephanie implied. 'Tony, or Michel?'

She met Stephanie's direct look with equanimity, glimpsed the momentary speculation before it was quickly masked and cast her a wicked smile.

'Surely you jest?'

Sandrine refrained from responding as Michel loomed close.

She felt her body stiffen in anticipation of his touch and she unconsciously held her breath, only releasing it when he made no attempt at physical contact.

'Michel, you've met Stephanie?' she managed smoothly.

'Yes. We shared an interesting discussion on marketing techniques.'

'Albeit that it was brief.'

'Something we will correct, *n'est-ce pas*?'

Oh, my, he was good. The right amount of interest, the desired element of charm, with hard business acumen just visible beneath the surface.

'It will be a pleasure,' Stephanie accorded, then she excused herself, and Sandrine watched as she talked briefly to Tony before exiting the room.

'She is a friend?'

The mildness of Michel's voice didn't deceive her. 'Actors have little to do with the business heads.'

'Am I to assume, then, that tonight is the first time you've met?'

She cast him a mocking glance. 'Would you like me to give you a run-down on everyone at this soiree? Whom I speak to, touch?' She paused a beat. 'Kiss?'

'Careful,' Michel warned silkily. 'You're treading dangerous ground.'

'In the name of one's craft, of course,' she added, and derived a degree of personal satisfaction at the way his eyes narrowed.

'If I thought otherwise,' he drawled, 'I'd carry you kicking and screaming onto the first plane out of here.'

'Neanderthal tactics belong to a distant civilisation.'

'Neanderthal and civilised do not mesh, *chérie*. Persist in baiting me, and I'll show you just how un-civilised I can be.'

Her chin lifted, and her eyes remained remarkably steady as they clashed with his. 'Too late, *mon amant*. I've already been there, remember?'

'I retain a vivid memory of a little wildcat who threw a few objects at me in temper.'

Expensive Waterford crystal. An inkwell, a paper-weight and a small clock decorating the antique desk in his study.

At the time she'd been too angry to care, but after-wards she'd experienced a pang of regret for the ex-quisite crystal items that formed part of a desk set. And the panelled wall they'd collided with before fall-ing to the marble floor to shatter in glittering shards when Michel deftly moved out of the line of fire.

Now, as she reviewed her explosive reaction, she

felt ashamed for having displayed such a lack of control.

'You provoked me.'

'It was reciprocal.'

Words. His, cool and controlled, whereas hers had been the antithesis of calm. Yet equally hurtful, uttered in frustrated anger.

'Space and time, Michel?' Sandrine queried with a trace of bitterness. 'In which to cool down and pretend it never happened?'

'I imagined we'd already resolved the situation.'

The gold flecks in her eyes became more pronounced as she held on to her anger. Twin flags of colour highlighted her cheekbones as the memory of the very physical sex they'd shared immediately afterwards came vividly to mind. On top of his magnificent antique desk. Hard, no-holds-barred sex, libidinous, barbaric and totally wild. Afterwards he'd cradled her close and carried her upstairs, bathed and gently towelled her dry, then he'd taken her to bed where he made exquisite love long into the night.

She'd waited until he'd fallen asleep, then she'd dressed, thrown clothes into a suitcase, penned a hastily scrawled note and left as the new day's dawn was lightening a shadowed grey sky.

'No.' The single negation emerged with quiet dignity. Sex…even very good sex, she amended, didn't resolve anything.

He had never felt so frustrated in his life when he discovered she'd left. If he could have, he'd have boarded the next Australia-bound flight and followed her. Except Raoul was in America, and Sebastian, youngest of the three Lanier brothers, was honeymooning overseas. He'd had no option but to attend scheduled meetings in various European cities, then conclude them with a brief family visit with his *grand-mère* in Paris.

'An empty space in bed, a brief note, and a wife on the other side of the world who refused to take any of my calls.' For that, he could have shaken her senseless.

'If you're through with the interrogation,' Sandrine said stiffly, 'I'd like to leave. I have an early call in the morning.'

His features hardened and his eyelids lowered slightly, successfully masking his expression. 'Then let's find our host and thank him for his hospitality.' He took hold of her arm, only to have her wrench it out of his grasp.

'I'm not going anywhere with you.'

One eyebrow arched in a deliberately cynical gesture. 'Are you forgetting our bargain so soon?'

'Not at all,' Sandrine declared bravely. 'But I'm damned if I'll allow you to share a house with me!'

His smile bore no humour at all. 'Separate residences aren't part of the deal.'

'Go to hell,' she vented, sorely tried.

'I've been there,' Michel said with dangerous softness. 'I don't intend a return trip.'

'I think,' she declared with controlled civility, 'we should save any further discussion until later.'

'I haven't even begun,' he stated with deliberate

emphasis. 'And the guests are free to speculate as they like.' He curved an arm around her waist and anchored her firmly to his side. 'Place one foot in front of the other and smile as we bid Tony goodnight.'

'*Or else*?' Sandrine countered with controlled anger.

'It's a matter of dignity. Yours,' Michel declared in a silky smooth tone. 'You can walk out of here or you can exit this apartment hoisted over my shoulder. Choose.'

Her stomach turned a slow somersault. One glance at his set features was sufficient to determine it wouldn't be wise to oppose him.

Her eyes held a chill that rivalled an arctic floe. 'I prefer the first option,' she said with icy politeness.

It took ten minutes to exchange pleasantries and have Michel confirm a business meeting with Tony the following morning. Sandrine didn't miss the slight tightness of Tony's smile or the fleeting hardness evident in his eyes.

'He's sweating on your decision,' she inferred as they rode the lift down to the ground floor. 'A calculated strategy, Michel?'

He sent a dark, assessing look in her direction, and she glimpsed a faint edge of mockery beneath the seemingly inscrutable veneer.

The query didn't require a verbal affirmation. The three Lanier brothers, Raoul, Michel and Sebastian, controlled a billion-dollar corporation spearheaded by their father, Henri, who had ensured each of his three sons' education encompassed every financial aspect of business.

The lift slid to a smooth halt, and they crossed the foyer to the main external entrance.

Sandrine extracted her cell phone and flipped it open. 'I'll call you a taxi.'

The streetlight nearby provided a luminous glow, the shadows highlighting the strong planes of his face.

'I have a hire-car,' Michel informed her silkily. 'I'll follow you.'

'You can move in tomorrow—' She broke off as the connection engaged. 'Could you send a cab to—'

Michel ended the call by the simple expediency of removing the small unit from her hand.

'How *dare* you?' The words spilled out in spluttered rage, and she made a valiant attempt to snatch the cell phone from him, failing miserably as he held it beyond her reach. 'Give it to me!'

One eyebrow arched in silent cynicism as she stamped her foot in wordless rage.

'Where are you parked?'

She glared at him balefully, incensed that much of her visual anger was diminished by the dark evening shadows. 'Aren't you booked in somewhere?'

She had tenacity, temper and *tendresse*. The latter had never been so noticeably absent. A faint twinge of humour tugged at the edge of his mouth. 'I checked out this morning.'

Damn, *damn* him, she silently vented. 'My car is the white Honda hatchback,' she told him in stilted tones. She turned away, only to have his hand snag her arm, and she whirled back to face him in vengeful fury. 'What now?'

'Your cell phone,' Michel said mildly as he held it out to her. She snatched it from him as if his fingers represented white-hot flame.

She would, she determined angrily as she slid in behind the wheel and engaged the engine, drive as fast as she dared and hope to lose him. Fat chance, Sandrine silently mocked minutes later as she ran an amber light and saw, via the rear-vision mirror, his car follow.

Knowing Michel's attention to detail, it wouldn't surprise her if he had already discovered her address and was therefore quite capable of reaching it with the aid of a street map. It was a sobering thought and one that relegated her actions to a foolish level.

No more taking risks with the traffic lights, she determined as she settled down to the twenty-minute drive and tried to ignore the twin set of headlights following several metres to the rear of her car.

Sandrine switched on the radio, selected a station at random and turned up the sound. Heavy rock music filled the interior, and she tried to lose herself in the beat, hoping it would distract her attention from Michel.

It didn't work, and after several minutes she turned down the sound and concentrated on negotiating a series of traffic roundabouts preceding the Sanctuary Cove turn-off.

A security gate guarded the entrance to the road leading to her waterfront villa, and she activated it, passed through, then followed the curving ribbon of bricked road past a clutch of low-rise apartment buildings until she reached her own.

After raising the garage door by remote control, she eased the car to a halt as Michel slid a sleek late-model sedan alongside her own.

The garage door closed, and Sandrine emerged from behind the wheel to see Michel pop the boot of his car and remove a set of luggage. She wanted to ignore him, but Michel Lanier wasn't a man you could successfully ignore.

Something twisted painfully in the pit of her stomach as she unlocked the door leading from the garage into the villa.

Pausing, she turned back towards him. 'There are three bedrooms upstairs,' she informed in a tone resembling that of a hostess instructing a guest. 'Choose one. There's spare linen in the cupboard.'

He didn't answer, and the silence was enervating. Without a further word, she stepped through to the hallway and made her way towards the kitchen.

The villa's interior was light and modern, with high ceilings and huge glass floor-to-ceiling windows. Large urns painted to blend with the muted peach-and-green colour scheme held a variety of artificial flowers and greenery, adding a tropical ambience to the expanse of marble-tiled floors.

The only sound was the staccato click of her stiletto heels as she crossed into the kitchen, and within minutes the coffee machine exuded an exotic aroma of freshly dripped brew.

Sandrine extracted two cups and saucers, sugar,

milk, placed them on the counter, then she filled one cup and took an appreciative sip.

It was quiet, far too quiet, and she crossed into the lounge and activated the television, switching channels until she found something of interest. The images danced, her vision unfocused as her mind wandered to the man who had invaded her home.

Temporary home, she corrected, aware that filming would wrap up within a week or two. Less for her, as she was only required in a few more scenes. Then what? Where would she go? There were a few options, and she mentally ticked them off. One, return to Sydney. Two, find modelling work. Three… No, she didn't want to think about the third option. A marriage should be about equality, sharing and understanding each other's needs. Domination of one partner by another was something she found unacceptable.

Sandrine finished her coffee, rinsed her cup, checked her watch, then released a heavy sigh. It was late, she was tired, and, she decided, she was damned if she'd wait any longer for Michel to put in an appearance. *She* was going to bed.

The silence seemed uncanny, and she found herself consciously listening for the slightest sound as she ascended the stairs. But there was none.

If Michel had showered, unpacked and made up a bed, he'd achieved it in a very short time.

The curved staircase led onto a semicircular, balustraded gallery. Three bedrooms, each with an en suite, were positioned along it, while the double doors at the head of the stairs opened to a spacious sitting room.

Sandrine turned right when she reached the top and entered the bedroom she'd chosen to use as her own. Soft lighting provided illumination, and her nostrils flared at the scent of freshly used soap and the lingering sharpness of male toiletries even as her eyes swivelled towards the large bed.

The elegant silk spread had been thrown back, and a long male frame lay clearly outlined beneath the light covering.

Michel. His dark head was nestled comfortably on the pillow, his eyes closed, his breathing slow and even.

Dammit, he was in *her* bed! Asleep!

Well, that would soon change, she decided furiously as she marched across the room. Without hesitation she picked up a spare pillow and thumped it down onto the mattress mere inches from his chest.

'Wake up,' she vented between clenched teeth. 'Damn you, wake up!' She lifted the pillow and brought it down for the second time. 'You're not staying in my room!'

He didn't move, and in a gesture of sheer frustration she pounded the pillow onto his chest.

A hand snaked out as she made to lift the pillow for another body blow, and she gasped as his fingers mercilessly closed over her forearm. Dark eyes seared hers.

'This is my room, my bed. And you're not occupying either.'

'You want a separate room, a separate bed?' His eyes seemed to shrivel her very soul. 'Go choose one.'

'You're doing this deliberately, aren't you?' she demanded, sorely tried. Pain focused behind each temple, and she lifted her hands to soothe the ache with her fingers. 'I'm not sleeping with you.'

'*Sleep* is the operative word,' Michel drawled.

She controlled the urge to hit him…by the skin of her teeth. 'You expect me to *believe* that?'

He looked…magnificent, and dangerous as hell. The brooding sexuality he exuded sent warning flares of heat racing through her veins.

Sandrine shifted her attention to his face and settled fleetingly on his mouth. Her lips quivered in vivid memory of how they'd moved beneath his own only a few hours ago. A traitorous warmth invaded her body, and she almost waived controlling it. *Almost.*

'Afraid to share the bed with me, Sandrine?'

Yes, she longed to cry. Because all it will take is the accidental brush of skin against skin in the night when I'm wrapped in sleep to forget for a few essential seconds, and then it'll be too late.

'Sex isn't going to make what's wrong between us right.'

'I don't recall suggesting that it would.'

'Then perhaps you'd care to explain why you've chosen my room, my *bed*?' she sputtered, indicating the bed, *him*. She drew in a deep breath, then released it slowly. 'If you had any gentlemanly instincts, you would have found another room!'

'I have never pretended to be a gentleman.'

Sandrine glared at him. 'No,' she agreed. 'Barbarian is more appropriate!'

'Careful, *chérie*,' Michel warned silkily.

A small decorative cushion lay within easy reach, and she swept it up in one hand and hurled it at him. 'I hate you.'

Two seconds later she lay pinned to the mattress as Michel loomed close above her. 'Let us put this *hate* to the test, hmm?'

She fought him, vainly twisting her body beneath his own as she attempted to wrench her hands free. 'Don't do this.'

It was a statement, not a plea, and he noted all her fine anger, her fearless tenacity and her passion. All it would take was subtle persuasion and sensual skill to have her become pliant in his arms.

'Then you should have thought before you pounded me with a pillow.'

'If you bait me, expect a reaction,' she launched in pithy response.

His expression didn't change although she could have sworn she glimpsed a glimmer of amusement.

'So...do you want to continue with this game of one-upmanship, or shall we bring it to a halt? Your call, Sandrine.'

She wanted to yell *Fight to the death*, and be damned. Except it would be *her* death. Emotionally, mentally, physically. And she didn't want to offer him that power.

'If you'll *move* yourself,' she suggested with expressive intonation, 'I'll go change and shower.'

'*Oui*, but first...' He took her mouth in a fleeting soft kiss, lingered at the edge, then swept his tongue into the silky interior to wreak brief and devastating havoc before easing his lengthy frame back onto the mattress. '*Bonne nuit, mignonne.*'

He rolled onto his side, pulled the covering to his waist and closed his eyes.

Sandrine lay frozen for a few seconds as she savoured the taste of him. Warm, musky and wickedly erotic. Damn him, she swore silently. He might have allowed her to call the tune, but he'd managed to have the last word.

With extreme care, she slid off the bed and crossed to the en suite, undressed, then took a leisurely shower, allowing the hot spray to ease the tension tightening her neck and shoulder muscles. Then she closed the dial, reefed a towel and, minutes later, donned a cotton nightshirt.

It seemed ironic and, she perceived wryly, probably owed something to her rebellious streak that she possessed complete sets of exquisite satin-and-lace French lingerie, yet alone she chose to wear something plain and functional to bed.

Michel lay still, his breathing deep and even as she crossed the room to snap off the light.

Afraid to share the bed with me? His words whispered in an unspoken challenge, taunting her.

Maybe she should turn the tables on him and do the unexpected. He'd sleep for hours, and although she wouldn't be there to witness it, she'd give almost anything to glimpse the look on his face when he woke and saw she'd occupied the other half of the bed.

A secret smile curved her lips as she slipped under the covers. He wanted to play games, huh? Well, let the games begin!

It gave her satisfaction to devise one scheme after another until sleep claimed her and tipped her into a world of dreams where Michel was alternately lover and devil, the location changed from one side of the world to another and became a film set where she was centre stage without any recollection of her lines.

CHAPTER THREE

SANDRINE came sharply awake to the shrilling sound of her digital alarm and automatically reached out a hand to turn it off. Except she was on the wrong side of the bed, and her fingers came into contact with a hard, warm male shoulder.

Michel. She tore her hand away as he uttered a muffled Gallic curse and reared into a sitting position.

'My alarm,' she explained sweetly as she slipped out of bed and crossed round to still the strident sound. The illuminated numerals registered four-thirty. 'Sorry if it woke you.'

She wasn't sorry at all. It was payback time for last night, and victory was sweet.

Drapes covered the wall of glass, filtering the early dawn light. This was Queensland, and the height of summer when the sun rose soon after four in the morning.

Sandrine crossed to the walk-in robe, selected jeans and a sleeveless ribbed top, then she collected fresh underwear and stepped into the adjoining en suite.

Ten minutes later she emerged, dressed, her face completely devoid of any make-up and her hair twisted into a loose knot at her nape.

She didn't give the bed or its occupant a single glance as she caught up her bag and exited the room.

In the kitchen she extracted fresh orange juice, drank it, then picked up a banana and made her way through to the garage.

Fifteen minutes later she was in make-up, mentally going over her lines while the wizard in cosmetic artistry began transforming her for the camera.

On reflection, it was not a happy day. Everyone was edgy, tempers flared as the temperature rose, and professionalism was strained to the limit.

It hadn't helped when Michel put in an appearance on the set after the lunch break. He stood in the background, his presence unquestioned given his possible investment, an apparently interested observer of the film-making process as the actors went through their paces...again and again as Tony sought perfection in his quest to impress.

No matter how hard Sandrine tried to ignore her indomitable husband, he was *there*, a constant on the edge of her peripheral vision, ensuring that her total focus was shot to hell.

'What are you doing here?' she demanded sotto voce during a break from filming.

Michel leant forward and brushed his lips to her temple. '*Chérie*, is that any way to greet your husband?'

'Please. Go away.'

She caught a glimpse of humour lurking at the edge of his mouth and bit back the need to scream.

'If I'm going to invest a considerable amount of money in order to salvage this venture,' he drawled, 'I think I should check out the action.'

'This is supposed to be a closed set.'

'I'm here at Tony's invitation.'

'Very cleverly baited, I imagine, so that our esteemed director took the hook?'

His smile didn't reach his eyes. 'You know me so well.'

No, she wanted to refute. I thought I did, but now I feel I hardly know you at all.

'How long do you intend to stay?'

'On the set? Until you finish for the day.' He lifted a hand and brushed gentle fingers across one cheek. 'Why? Does my presence bother you?'

She sharpened her verbal claws. 'Isn't that your purpose?'

'Shouldn't you read through your lines?' Michel countered, watching as she turned without a word and crossed to pick up her copy of the script.

It didn't help any that Cait London chose that moment to exert her considerable feminine charm or that Michel appeared responsive, albeit politely so.

A ploy to make her jealous? It's working, isn't it? a wretched little imp taunted.

She watched them surreptitiously beneath veiled lashes and had to admit the blood simmered in her veins as Cait flirted outrageously with the deliberate touch of her hand on his sleeve, the wickedly sensual smile, the brazen *knowledge* evident in those glittering blue eyes.

Sandrine felt the knot in her stomach tighten as she sightlessly scanned the upcoming scene in her copy of the script.

Damn Michel. For every darn thing. And especially for invading her professional turf.

'Okay, everyone. Places, please.'

Thank heavens for small mercies, Sandrine accorded as she mentally prepared herself to be in character and silently rehearsed her few lines.

It was late afternoon before Sandrine was dismissed from the set with the news she wouldn't be required until Tuesday. The person responsible for continuity took the requisite Polaroid, and Sandrine went through the process of discarding the elegant costume and wig with help from the wardrobe assistant, then she removed her make-up and shook her hair free from the confining hairnet.

The comparison between screen actress in character and the modern jean-clad girl was remarkable. So remarkable, she decided ruefully, that it was unlikely anyone would recognise her as being one and the same person.

It was after five when she emerged into the parking lot, and she filched keys from her carry-bag as she walked towards her car.

'Hoping to slip away undetected?'

Michel fell into step beside her, and she quickened her pace, choosing not to answer him.

A minute later she slipped the key into the lock and opened the door, then slid in behind the wheel and fired the engine.

A great exit line would have been *Eat my dust*, except the moment was dramatically reduced as her tyres squealed faintly on smooth bitumen, and she was forced to adhere to the low speed limit.

However, once she hit the highway she put her foot down and let the speedometer needle soar as far as she dared without risk to life or limb or threat of a speeding ticket. It provided some release for the build-up of tension.

Sandrine reached Sanctuary Cove in record time, and inside the villa she ran lightly upstairs, changed into a maillot, grabbed a towel, retraced her steps and went out to the pool.

The water was refreshingly cool, and she stroked several lengths of the pool before turning onto her back and lazily allowing the buoyancy of the water keep her afloat.

It was all too easy to allow her thoughts to wander and reflect on the day's events.

And Michel.

She hadn't slept well and had spent much of her waking hours wondering at her sanity in sharing the same bed. It was madness, an act that amounted to masochism. For to lie so close, yet be so far from him, attacked her emotional foundation and tore it to shreds.

What would he have done if she'd reached out and touched him? If he'd ignored her, she'd have died. Yet if he'd responded, how could she hope to handle the aftermath?

Such an act could only amount to sexual gratification and achieve nothing except provide mutual satisfaction. Akin to scratching an itch.

The attuning of heart, mind and soul would be missing, and somehow just *sex* wasn't enough.

She was mad. Insane, she added mentally. Any other woman would catch hold of Michel's coat-tails, exult in all that his wealth and social prestige could provide and hang in there for the ride.

And what a ride! Even the thought of it sent warmth flooding through her body. Each separate nerve end quivered in anticipation, and sensation wreaked havoc with her equilibrium.

It had been bad enough when they were oceans apart. Now that he was here, it was a thousand times worse.

Magic, she thought. Highly sensitised, sensual sorcery of a kind that defied valid description. Transmuted in the touch, the look, the promise…and the anticipation.

To part after a long night of loving and count each hour until they could be together again. To counter and feed that need with a phone call, a softly spoken promise. The delivery of a single red rose. That special look lovers exchange in a room filled with people. And the waiting, the wanting.

Was it love? The to-die-for, till-death-us-do-part kind of loving? Or was it sexual satiation, a sensual nirvana?

She'd thought it was both until their first serious argument. Now she wasn't so sure.

'Pleasant thoughts, I trust?'

The faintly inflected drawl caused her to jackknife

and turn towards the tall male figure standing close to the pool's edge.

Michel had discarded his jacket and tie and loosened the top two buttons of his shirt. His hair looked slightly ruffled, as if he'd dragged impatient fingers through its groomed length.

'How long have you been standing there?' she demanded.

'Does it matter?'

Watching her unobserved almost amounted to an invasion of privacy, and she didn't like it one bit.

A few strokes brought her to the side of the pool, and she levered herself easily to sit on its edge. Her towel lay out of reach on a lounger, and she rose to her feet, then caught it up in one quick movement.

His faint amusement didn't go unnoticed, and she determinedly blotted the excess moisture from her body before tending to her hair.

'I've booked a table for dinner at the Hyatt.'

Sandrine heard the words but momentarily chose to ignore them.

'I'm sure you'll enjoy the meal,' she managed calmly. 'I've heard the chef has an excellent reputation.'

'For two,' Michel informed her. 'At seven.'

'I shan't wait up.'

'You have an hour to shower and get ready.'

She looked at him steadily. 'I'm not going anywhere with you.'

'Damn, you try my patience!'

'And you try mine!'

'Is it unacceptable to want to share a meal with my wife in pleasant surroundings?'

'No,' Sandrine said sweetly. 'Providing your wife is willing. And in this instance, she's not!'

'Sandrine—'

'Don't threaten me, Michel.' She tried for quiet dignity but didn't quite make it. Her eyes speared his, dark and intense with emotion. 'I refuse to fall in with every suggestion you make.'

'You prefer to eat here?'

'Don't you get it? I don't want to share a meal with you. *Anywhere.*' A faint tremor shook her body, and she tightened her grip on the towel.

His eyes narrowed. 'You're shivering.'

'How perceptive,' she mocked. 'If you'll excuse me, I'll go take a hot shower.' As she moved past him, she endeavoured to ignore the sheer magnetism of the man. And her body's traitorous reaction.

Two more weeks, she reasoned as she ran lightly upstairs. Maybe less. And filming would be over. At least, her participation would finish. Could she go the distance, living in the same villa, sharing the same bed as the man who was bent on using any advantage he could gain?

Sandrine reached her bedroom and crossed into the adjoining en suite. A swift turn of the dial and warm water cascaded onto the tiled floor of the shower.

It took only seconds to strip the wet Lycra from her body, and she stepped into the large cubicle, reached for the bottle of shampoo, then began the task of lathering it through her hair.

Ten minutes later she emerged into the bedroom and came to a sudden halt at the sight of Michel in the process of discarding his clothes.

'Finished?'

Sandrine's left hand flew to the towel carelessly caught in a knot between her breasts, and with her right she steadied the towel wound high on her head.

'There are two other bathrooms on this level,' she pointed out in a slightly strangled voice.

'You object to sharing?'

Oh, my, he was good. Reasonable, faintly teasing beneath the edge of cynicism.

'Yes,' she returned, regaining her equilibrium as she crossed the room to collect fresh underwear. 'Considering your main purpose is to unsettle me.'

'An admission I'm succeeding, Sandrine?'

She'd fallen straight into that one, hadn't she? 'Not at all,' she responded calmly, and knew she lied. Her entire nervous system jangled at the very thought of him.

Watching Michel as he crossed the room to the bathroom created a havoc all of its own as she took in his broad frame, the muscular set of his shoulders, superb pectorals, the hard-packed diaphragm and firm waist.

She controlled a faint shiver at the thought of what it felt like to be held close, to feel the strength in those arms as he enfolded her firmly within them.

It was almost possible to breathe in the musky aroma of his skin, the clean freshness of the soap he used, the male cologne. Sense the way he tasted when her mouth joined with his, the faintly abrasive and moist slide as their tongues caressed and explored in an erotic mating dance.

The essence of his sex, the degree of power she experienced in taking him to the brink of his control, the way that large male body shook as he tumbled over the edge. Man at his most vulnerable.

Sandrine tried to restrain the way heat flared through her body, but she failed as the image of his lovemaking rose to taunt her.

He had the look, the touch, the power to drive a woman wild. And much to her chagrin, there was a part of her that wanted him badly. Without question or recrimination.

She heard the faint buzz of his electric razor, followed minutes later by the fall of water in the shower stall.

She immediately visualised Michel's naked form, his potent masculinity, the impressive power sheathed at the apex of his thighs.

Focus, concentrate, *remember* the accusations they'd exchanged seven weeks ago, she silently raged as she discarded the towel and stepped into briefs, then fastened her bra before pulling on a pair of jeans and a cotton top.

That fateful night she had looked at Michel... someone she'd loved with all her heart, in whom she had implicit trust, and believed their lives, their love, were forever entwined...and now it was like looking at a stranger.

With an irritated gesture, Sandrine unwound the

towel from her head and shook out hair that fell in a cloud of sable silk onto her shoulders.

How did the axiom go? *Marry in haste, repent at leisure*?

She reached for the hair dryer, plugged it in, then began combing the warm air through her hair.

What would have happened if she'd stayed? If she'd cancelled her flight and risked a breach of contract? Would they have resolved anything? Or had her abrupt departure merely precipitated their separation?

Seven weeks. Weeks that could be viewed as a brief respite, or a lifetime, depending on the interpretation.

'You intend wearing casual gear to dinner?'

Sandrine reached forward and switched off the hair dryer. Via mirrored reflection, she saw him discard the towel, step into briefs, then pull on tailored trousers before crossing to the wardrobe and extracting a shirt.

'I hadn't planned on dressing up.' She caught her hair and began winding it into a knot.

'Leave it loose.'

Her hands didn't falter as she fastened the knot with pins. 'It's cooler if I wear it up.'

Michel buttoned his shirt, fastened his trousers, then pulled on socks and shoes.

'No make-up?'

'Why?' Sandrine countered. 'I'm not planning on going anywhere.'

His expression didn't change, but his eyes hardened. 'I leave in five minutes, Sandrine. With, or without you. Your choice.'

She turned to face him. 'You could always ring

Cait. She'd just *die* to share anything with you.'
Without a further word, she walked from the room and
made her way downstairs to the kitchen.

A tin of salmon and a tossed salad were poor sub-
stitutes for the appetiser, main course, fruit and cheese
board Michel would no doubt enjoy with table service,
a fine wine, subdued lighting and soft background music. She told herself she didn't care as she heard him
exit the house, followed by the start of a car engine.

Half an hour later she rinsed the few plates she'd
used, placed them in the dishwasher, then filled a glass
with bottled water and crossed into the lounge to
watch television.

At ten she dimmed the lights and went upstairs to
bed. For a few minutes she dithered over *which* bed,
rationalising that the main bedroom was *hers*, and if
Michel was determined to make it *his*, then he could
damn well *suffer* because she didn't intend to move.

Yet sharing the bed was akin to playing with fire,
and no way did she want to get burned. To slip into
the convenience of pleasurable sex wasn't on her
agenda.

With that thought in mind she collected linen and
made up the bed in a room farthest from the one
Michel had designated his own. Then she moved a few
essentials in clothes and toiletries and determinedly
slid between cool percale sheets, then turned out the
light.

Moonlight shone through in between the painted
wooden shutters, and after what seemed an intermi-

nable length of time spent tossing and turning, she padded across to the window to adjust them.

Sleep was never more distant, and she did the yoga thing, counted sheep and endeavoured to think pleasant, relaxing thoughts. Except the image that rose to taunt her belonged to Michel, and she rolled onto her stomach and punched the pillow.

Her room faced the water and was therefore at the opposite end of the house to the garage. Was he home yet? She hadn't heard so much as a sound to indicate he'd returned.

Maybe some gorgeous female had insisted on sharing his table and right this minute they were caught up in a web of harmless seduction. Or would it be harmless? Michel was a practised raconteur, and charm personified. He also possessed an indefinable sensual aura that had most women conjuring up every ploy in the book to attract his attention.

Sandrine played numerous different scenarios in her mind, damning Michel in every one of them until her subconscious mind took her deeper into vivid dreams that seemed no less real.

It was after eleven when the powerful car whispered to a halt in the garage. Michel entered the house and turned out lights as he gained the upper floor.

The empty bed gave him a bad moment, then he systematically conducted a quiet search of the remaining rooms and experienced an enormous degree of relief when he discovered his wife's recumbent form caught in a tangled twist of sheets.

He stood in the open doorway for several long minutes, then crossed to the bed.

She was beautiful. So fiercely independent and possessed of so much spirit. He wanted to smooth the hair back from her forehead and brush his lips across her temple.

Damn. He wanted more, so much more than a gesture of tenderness. He craved what they'd once shared. The mesmeric magical heat that culminated in shameless passion and encapsulated them as twin halves of a whole. Complete, inviolate, *one* on every level... spiritually mentally, emotionally.

Another curse whispered from his lips, one that would have scorched the ears of anyone who chanced to overhear it. Directed entirely at himself for allowing the strictures of business to take precedence over love for his wife.

Instead of taking the next flight in pursuit, he'd thrown himself into resolving extremely delicate financial negotiations in a takeover bid integral to the family's overflowing coffers. And ensured Sandrine's safety by employing a pair of highly reputable professionals to watch over her twenty-four hours a day.

His manipulative skill in the business arena was highly regarded among his peers. Women actively pursued him for his wealth and social position. They pandered to his ego, made all the right practised moves in an existence that he'd come to consider artificial. Experience had made him both cynical and wary.

Until Sandrine.

Sandrine, with her lack of guile and artifice, whose

laughter was both infectious and earthy. Her smile could light up her whole body so that her skin glowed and her eyes gleamed with a reflected warmth that came straight from the heart.

He'd wanted her from that first moment, not just in the biblical sense. Instinct warned it would be more than that. Much more.

She was his most precious possession, and from the beginning he'd wanted to shield and protect her.

There was no way he could sanction her flying off to the other side of the world without him. Or staying there alone. The timing, given his professional responsibility, couldn't have been worse.

A wry smile twisted his mouth. Financial wizardry was his speciality, and fate had been on his side. He could rescue a movie on the brink of foundering and employ emotional blackmail to salvage his marriage. What was it they said? *Kill two birds with one stone.*

The movie didn't present a problem. Sandrine, on the other hand, would be no easy victory.

It was a challenge. The most important of his life, and one he was determined to win.

A slight sound caught his attention, and he watched as she turned restlessly onto her back.

She looked defenceless in sleep, he mused. Her skin smooth and translucent in the reflected hall light. Her eyelashes impossibly long, and her mouth soft and lushly curved.

His emotions stirred into life, and he determinedly tamped them down as he gathered her into his arms and carried her back to the room they'd shared the previous night.

She stirred slightly as he lowered her into bed, then she settled, and he removed his clothes and slid in beside her to lie silent and unmoving in the darkness until sleep finally claimed him long after the witching hour of midnight.

CHAPTER FOUR

SANDRINE woke slowly as gradual awareness dispensed one layer of unconsciousness after another, bringing with it the reality of a new day.

Sunday, she determined with a restful sigh. No early-morning call, no studio.

Then she remembered, and with memory came the realisation that she wasn't in the bed or the room she'd retreated to last night.

What's more, she wasn't alone.

A masculine arm held her anchored closely against a very male frame. A very aroused male.

Michel's hand splayed over her stomach, and she could feel his steady, rhythmic heartbeat against her shoulder.

Dear God.

Seeking help from the Deity didn't work. Nor did the fervent but faint hope she might be dreaming, for no one dreamed with their eyes open.

Her thoughts reflected a kaleidoscope of conflicting emotions as she rationalised what action she should take.

If she kept her breathing even and she moved slowly, an inch at a time, maybe Michel wouldn't notice, and eventually she'd be able to slip free from his grasp and the bed.

A ridiculous strategy, she silently castigated herself seconds later when the slightest movement resulted in an involuntary tightening of his hold.

What now? Jab her elbow into his ribs? Thump a fist against his forearm? Maybe both? Yes, that might work.

'Planning your method of attack?' a deep voice drawled far too close to one ear.

'You got it in one,' she responded thickly, aiming a vicious jab with her elbow...and missed as he successfully deflected the manoeuvre. Kicking her heel against his shins didn't make an impression at all, and she uttered a growl in rage. 'Let me go!'

'*S'il vous plaît*?' he queried musingly.

'Go to hell.'

'If you want to play...'

'You're enjoying this, aren't you?' she retorted vengefully as she twisted helplessly to free herself.

'Not particularly. I prefer a woman to be pliant and willing in my arms.'

'Fat chance!'

'You would like me to prove how easily I can change your mind?'

Sandrine lay very still as she attempted to control the sudden hitch in her breathing. All too easily, she agreed silently, much to her chagrin.

He buried his mouth in the soft curve of her neck, then trailed a path to her temple. His hand moved up to cup her breast, and her stomach muscles tightened against the onslaught of sensation.

'Is this where you insist I fulfil my part of the bargain?'

With one easy movement he rolled onto his back and carried her with him to straddle his waist. His features were dark, accentuated by the visible evidence of a night's growth of beard. His eyes held a watchful quality, assessing and vaguely analytical.

This, *this*, she qualified shakily, could prove highly dangerous.

He resembled a lazy tiger, supine, visually content, but exuding a primitive degree of power. One wrong word or move on her part and she entertained no doubt his indolent facade would swiftly vanish.

Her position was extremely tenuous, to say the least.

He lifted a hand and brushed the back of his fingers down her cheek, then slid them forward to cup her chin. 'Your definition, not mine.'

He pressed his thumb against the centre of her lower lip, and acute sensation quivered through her body. 'I moved into another room by choice.'

'And I brought you back here.'

'Because you don't like sleeping alone?' she queried with deliberate sarcasm.

'Sex isn't necessarily a prerequisite to sharing the nuptial bed.'

'You expect me to believe that? Of *you*?'

He was silent for several telling seconds, and when he spoke his voice was so silky it sent shivers scudding down the length of her spine. 'I have a vivid memory of the long nights we shared, *chérie*.'

So did she. Nights when she became a willing wanton in his arms as she embraced a sensual feast so erotic there were times when she wept from the joy of it.

'That was then,' Sandrine said slowly, and glimpsed his wry smile.

'And this is now, hmm?'

'Yes.'

'In that case, let's get dressed and go downstairs for breakfast.' In one smooth movement he lifted her to stand on the floor, then he swept aside the covers and slid to his feet.

Clothes, bathroom, she decided, in that order, gathering jeans and a stretch rib-knit top. Seconds later she was safely ensconced behind a closed door with, she hoped, total privacy.

There were no locks on the internal doors, and she took a quick shower, dressed, then emerged to find the bedroom empty.

Sandrine descended the stairs and followed the aroma of freshly brewed coffee to the kitchen, where Michel looked completely at ease breaking eggs into a bowl while a skillet heated on the stove top. Dressed in black designer jeans and a white polo-neck knit shirt, he looked indecently male.

His actions reminded her of the breakfasts they'd shared and their easy camaraderie. Then, she would have teased him mercilessly, applauded his skill and uttered a husky laugh as he carried her back to the bedroom.

Now, she silently filled two glasses with orange

juice, poured the coffee and transferred everything onto the table.

Michel placed one plate with a steaming omelette before her, then settled in the seat opposite.

Her stomach felt as if it were tied in knots, and it irked her considerably that his appetite didn't appear in the least affected.

Sandrine forked a few morsels into her mouth, bit off a segment of toast, then sipped the strong black coffee.

Michel refilled his cup, added sugar, then pushed his empty plate to one side and sank back in his chair. 'We have the day. What do you suggest we do with it?'

She replaced her cup on its saucer and met his steady gaze with equanimity. 'I plan to go shopping.'

'Specifically?'

'Food,' she answered succinctly. 'Staples such as bread, milk, eggs, fruit.'

'And then?'

'Take the car and explore a little.'

Michel rose to his feet and began clearing the table. 'I'll drive. You can play navigator.'

'Excuse me?'

He cast her a musing glance that held a hint of patient forbearance. 'We'll take in the supermarket, then explore.'

'Since when did *I* become *we*?'

His silence was telling, his expression equally so, and she was the one to break his gaze as she gathered up a few spreads and carried them to the refrigerator.

'What if I'd prefer to be alone?'

'Don't push it, Sandrine.'

It took only minutes to rinse and stack the few plates in the dishwasher, then Sandrine collected her shoulder-bag, slid sunglasses atop her head and walked through to the garage, uncaring whether Michel followed or not.

Sanctuary Cove village comprised a wide variety of up-market stores and trendy boutiques, numerous cafés and restaurants and was accessed via two bricked lanes whose median strip held immaculately trimmed palm trees. The adjoining grounds fringed a lush green golf course, which seasonally hosted international competitions.

The few grocery staples required to boost supplies could have been selected in five minutes, but Sandrine deliberated over the choice of fruit, the varieties of lettuce, and opted to visit the local bakery rather than select packaged sliced bread.

Michel added a few selections of his own and appeared mildly amused when she rejected more than one.

Half an hour later they retreated to the villa, stored their purchases and returned to the car.

'Where to?'

'There are mountains, beaches, theme parks,' Sandrine responded as Michel eased the car through the security gate. 'Your choice.'

'Noosa.'

She cast him a startled glance. 'That's more than a two-hour drive north.'

He gave a slight shrug. 'Is that a problem?'

'No, I guess not.'

He reached a large roundabout and circled it. 'Navigate, Sandrine.'

She directed him onto the multilane highway where they joined the swift flow of traffic travelling north, and after an hour they took the Sunshine Coast bypass.

Soon they were driving through farmland devoted to sugarcane, avocados, pineapples, strawberries and a variety of fruit trees. Small country towns reflected a slower-paced lifestyle, old-style buildings mingling with modern, and in the distance lay the brooding range of bush-clad hills, a deep blue-green against the azure skyline.

'The Glasshouse Mountains,' Sandrine revealed, studying the tour-guide booklet. 'Montville, Maleny. Craft ware, quaint teashops, picturesque.'

'We'll go there tomorrow.'

She frowned and cast him a quick glance. It was difficult to determine anything from his expression for his eyes were shaded by dark sunglasses and his focus was on the road ahead.

'What do you mean...*tomorrow*?' she demanded.

'We'll detour through on the way back to the Coast,' Michel explained patiently.

'You intend for us to stay overnight in Noosa?'

'Is that a problem?'

'You're darn right it's a problem. I don't have a change of clothes for a start,' she said heatedly.

'It's a tourist strip. The shops will be open. We'll buy what we need.'

She turned on him with ill-concealed anger. 'Did you plan this?'

'It seems foolish to travel back to the Coast tonight, only to turn around and return again tomorrow,' he said reasonably.

'You could have asked me!'

'And given you the opportunity to refuse?'

She shot him a fulminating glare. 'I dislike being hijacked.'

'Look on it as an adventure.'

Some adventure! If she managed to get through the next thirty-six hours without hitting him, it would be a miracle.

'If I'd known you had this in mind, I'd have brought along the script. It might have escaped your attention, but I'm due on the set Tuesday and I need to study my lines!'

'I have it on good authority the lines are few, and unless the scene needs to be reshot, you should be done by midday.'

'I hate you.'

'Hate is a strong emotion and, as such, better than indifference.'

'You just missed the turn-off.'

'Caused by a navigational distraction?' he mocked as he decelerated, then swung the car into a wide turn.

Her lips tightened, and she refrained from uttering a further word except for curt, explicit instructions.

Michel chose the most up-market hotel resort on the main Hastings Street strip, relinquished the vehicle for valet parking, then led her into the main foyer to register.

It would serve him right if the hotel was fully booked, she reflected vengefully. Luck wasn't on her side as Michel completed the necessary paperwork and accepted a card folder with their room security tags.

Their suite overlooked the river towards a bank of riverfront mansions, Sandrine discovered on crossing to the window. The tranquil vista exuded a different ambience from that of the Gold Coast.

'Lunch,' Michel declared. 'Let's go find a place to eat.'

Sandrine turned towards him. 'I don't want to be part of a game you've chosen to play.'

'Specifically?'

'You're a superb tactician, Michel,' she acknowledged dryly.

'Is that a compliment, or a condemnation?'

'Both.'

'*Merci*,' he returned with wry humour. 'What game is it you imagine I'm playing?'

'One of revenge.'

He didn't pretend to misunderstand. 'Choosing to keep you in suspense as to when I begin collecting on our deal?'

'Yes.'

He wanted to cross the room and shake her until she pleaded for mercy. Instead, he thrust a hand into his trouser pocket and controlled the timbre of his voice. 'What if I said *tonight*?'

Something inside her stomach curled into a hard, painful ball. 'Why wait? Why not now?'

She reached for the buttons on her blouse and slowly undid one, then the other, forcing her fingers to remain steady until all the buttons were freed.

'Do you have any specific requirements?' Dear heaven, how could she sound so calm when inside she was shaking like a leaf?

'Enlighten me.'

'You're the one calling the shots.' She slid the blouse off one shoulder, then the other, and draped it carelessly over a nearby chair. As her fingers went to the snap fastening on her jeans, she looked over at him. 'Aren't you going to get out of your clothes?'

How far would she go? 'When you're done,' Michel drawled, calling her bluff, 'you can undress me.'

Pain arrowed through her body, so acute it almost made her wince. *Act*, a tiny voice prompted. You're good at it.

Sandrine managed a faint shrug. 'If that's what turns you on.' She slid the zip down on her jeans and slowly eased the denim over her hips. She slipped off her joggers, lifted one leg free, then the other, and tossed the jeans on top of the blouse.

He wasn't going to let her go through with this, was he?

She stood in briefs and bra, and although they covered her more adequately than a bikini, she felt vulnerable and exposed.

He stood perfectly still, his gaze steady and unblinking as she looked at him.

Damn him, he wasn't going to help her out.

With slow, sure steps she crossed to where he stood. His shirt was short-sleeved with three buttons at the neck. She caught hold of the knit fabric on either side of his rib cage and pulled it free from his waistband. Then she tugged upwards with little success until he obligingly raised his arms and lowered his head to accommodate the shirt's easy removal.

Too much. He really was much too much, she muttered silently. The spread of his shoulders, the breadth of chest, the strong musculature that rippled and bunched with every movement.

She threw the shirt in the path of her blouse and jeans, then turned back and reached for the snap on his jeans, pulled it open, then stifled a soft curse.

Buttons. No zip for easy unfastening.

Each one presented a fresh torture. Her fingers fumbled, and she felt totally inadequate for the task. It didn't help any that the denim was stretched tight against a hard male arousal.

She could, she reasoned, literally throw up her hands and tell him to complete the task himself. Except she was darned if she'd allow him the satisfaction of winning a challenge. She could almost hear his musing drawl, see the faint mockery in those dark eyes as he finished discarding his clothes.

As he would, if only to witness her discomfort, she determined as she dealt with another button.

How things had changed, she reflected wryly. In the not-too-distant past she'd have laughed and delighted in the task, taking pleasure in teasing him outrageously and exulting in his reaction.

Now, he had control while she slipped into such a state of nerves she couldn't even manage something as simple as undoing a series of buttons!

Just do it, the tiny voice urged. Slip into pretend mode and imagine he's someone who means nothing to you.

There, it was done. Stretch fashion jeans possessed one inescapable flaw. They were the very devil for someone else to remove! Tailored trousers wouldn't have presented any problem, but jeans were a different story, she decided, gritting her teeth as she tugged the fabric down over powerful thighs.

The action brought her face close to a vulnerable part of his anatomy, and she entertained the brief vindictive thought that with one quick movement she could cause him considerable pain. The consequences, however, wouldn't be worth it.

In a few swift movements he slid off his joggers, then stepped out of his jeans and kicked them to one side. Fine black silk skimmed his hips and couched his manhood, emphasising olive skin roughened by hair and a male frame in superb physical shape.

Sandrine momentarily closed her eyes, then opened them again. Michel wasn't an unknown lover. Why hesitate?

There was a part of her that longed for the feel of his mouth, the tactile skill of those clever hands as they created havoc with each separate pleasure zone. She wanted to lose herself in the wealth of emotional and spiritual sensations, to go to that special place where there was only *him*…and the unique alchemy they shared.

It had been good. Better than good, she amended.

A hand caught hold of her chin, lifted it so she had to look at him. His thumb traced the edge of her jaw, lingered there, then slid slowly down the column of her throat.

Sandrine swallowed compulsively, wanting to move away but held mesmerised by the darkness of those deep grey eyes as he forced her to hold his gaze.

Then he lowered his head and angled his mouth over hers in a kiss that was hard and mercilessly plundering as he took what she wouldn't willingly give.

Just as she thought her jaw would break, the pressure eased, and his tongue caressed and cajoled in a teasing dance that almost made her weep.

Not content, he savoured the taste of her lips, their soft, swollen contours throbbing beneath his touch. He nipped the full centre with the edge of his teeth, caught her indrawn breath, then angled his mouth to hers in a kiss that tore at the very threads of her soul.

With considerable ease his lips trailed a path down her neck, lingered as he explored the hollows at the edge of her throat, then travelled to the soft fullness of her breast.

In one easy movement he freed the twin hooks of her bra and dispensed with it before returning his attention to the rounded curve.

A soft flick from the tip of his tongue brought a

surge of sensation, and she arched her neck, allowing him access.

Her whole body began to melt as heat flowed through her veins, warming her body until she was on fire with a passion so strong, so tumultuous, there was only the man and the aching, wanting *need*.

His hand slid down to her waist, then splayed low over her stomach, his fingers slipping beneath the satin and lace of her briefs, seeking, probing, *teasing*, until she scaled the heights, clung, then descended in a free-falling spiral.

He caught her as she fell, held her, then took her on a return journey that was even more devastating than the first.

This time she was unable to still the soft, throaty cries or stop the flow of tears as they trickled slowly down her cheeks.

Michel brushed a thumb against each rivulet in turn, dispensing the dampness with a tenderness that brought a lump to her throat. His lips settled at the corner of her mouth, caressing the soft fullness of her lower lip with the edge of his tongue.

He paused to nibble the moist inner tissue, then conducted a seductive foray, tracing her tongue with his own, before taking possession with claim-staking action.

Sandrine was barely conscious of her hands creeping up to link together at his nape as he folded her close, and she kissed him back, giving, taking, in what became a storm of sensual exploration.

It wasn't enough. Not nearly enough, and she

moved against him, instinctively seeking more. Her hands shifted to his shoulders, then slid down over his back, urging him closer as she unconsciously raked her nails over muscled flesh to emphasise her need.

Without missing a beat, Michel swung an arm beneath her thighs and swept her into his arms, then tumbled with her down onto the bed. In one easy movement he rolled her beneath him, caging her body as he tore his briefs free.

It was as if every pore of her skin became highly sensitised to his touch, and an exigent sexual chemistry was apparent—vital, electric, lethal—for it melted her mental resistance, leaving only the craving for physical release.

Now, she urged, unaware whether the word left her lips or not. She was burning up inside, on fire with a primal heat so intense she lost sight of who and where she was in the need to have him deep inside her, matching each primeval movement until that deep, rhythmic possession transported them both simultaneously to exquisite sensual sensation.

Sandrine almost cried out loud when his mouth left hers and began a slow, tortuous descent, pausing to savour delicate hollows at the base of her throat before trailing a path to her breast, suckling first one acutely sensitised peak before delivering a similar assault on its twin.

Her stomach tensed as he explored the delicate indentation of her navel, and she gasped as he moved low to caress the most sensitive pleasure spot of all.

Her body arched as she became consumed by a

wicked ecstasy so acute she began to plead, muted guttural sounds she didn't recognise as being her own voice.

She reached for his head, seeking purchase on his hair, and she pulled it mercilessly in a bid to have him desist. Only to have him catch hold of her wrists and effortlessly clamp them to her sides.

'Michel.' His name emerged endless minutes later, accompanied by a mindless, tortured sob. 'Please.'

Seconds later he slowly raised his head and gave her a long, impassioned look. His eyes were so incredibly dark they were almost black.

Her breath came in ragged gasps, and her pulse seemed to beat so fast it was almost out of control. Her eyes felt too big for her face, their expression wild, dilated with an emotion she didn't care to define.

When his head lowered, she gave an anguished cry and felt her flesh quiver uncontrollably as he began bestowing an agonisingly slow trail of soft, open-mouthed kisses to her navel, the soft slope of her breasts, their tender aureoles, the slender column of her neck, before taking possession of her mouth.

Timeless minutes later he freed her hands, and the breath stilled in her throat as he entered her with one powerful thrust.

She could feel herself stretching to accommodate his length, the tightness as she enclosed and held him, followed by the primitive rhythm that he kept erotically slow at first, so measured and deep she was aware of every muscle contraction.

She was almost falling apart when he quickened the

pace to a heavy, pulsating action that took her so high she became wild with the force and strength of it.

Her body felt as if it were a finely tuned instrument played by a virtuoso until it was wooed to such a fine crescendo that the only possible climax was to fracture and splinter into a thousand pieces in the accompanying electric silence.

He remained buried deep inside her as he cradled her face and kissed the teardrops trickling slowly down each cheek, trailing their path to the edge of her lips.

How was it possible to weep with such a combination of acute pleasure and sadness? Sadness, she rationalised, for an awareness that the pleasure had been all hers.

Michel supported his weight, then bestowed a series of butterfly kisses to the contours of her mouth before lifting his head to gaze down at her.

'Okay?' he queried gently.

What could she say? There wasn't one adequate word that came readily to mind. 'Speechless,' she managed at last.

'I meant *you*,' he qualified slowly.

'Fine.' You lie, the tiny voice chastised. Your body still vibrates from the feel of him, and you ache with a hurt that has little to do with physical pain.

Michel saw the faint clouding evident in those beautifully luminous brown eyes and glimpsed the rapid pulse beat at the base of her throat.

He leant forward and placed his lips to that frenetically beating hollow, felt her tremor and gently tucked a stray swath of hair from her cheek.

Sandrine wanted to close her eyes and block out the sight of him, but that wasn't an option. Instead, she wrinkled her nose at him in silent, mocking remonstrance.

'Lunch,' she declared. 'I'm hungry.' In one easy movement she slid off the bed and crossed the room to the en suite.

Michel followed and merely arched an eyebrow when she lifted a hand in mute denial that he share her shower.

'Modesty is inappropriate,' he drawled as he stepped in beside her, caught up the soap and began lathering it over her body.

'Give it to me,' she said in a strangled voice as she attempted to take the soap from his hand.

'No.'

She didn't want to fight. Dammit, she didn't possess the energy or the inclination right at this moment to do more than submit to his ministrations.

When he finished, she let the fine needle spray rinse the soap from her body, then she slid open the glass door and reached for a towel. By the time Michel emerged she was dressed, her hair was swept into a knot on top of her head, and she was applying colour to her lips.

He pulled on his clothes, ran his fingers through his dampened hair, then he inclined his head in bemused mockery and swept an arm towards the door. 'After you.'

CHAPTER FIVE

THEY selected a small intimate restaurant with an appealing blackboard menu, chose an outdoor table shaded by a large umbrella, ordered seafood pasta, *focaccia* and white wine, and were impressed by the quality of the food and the service.

Sandrine declined anything to follow and settled for strong black coffee.

'You enjoyed the food?'

She looked at the man seated opposite and fought against an enveloping wave of sensation.

How was it that he had this cataclysmic effect on her? He exuded an unfair share of sensuality, an inherent quality that was both mesmeric and magical.

'Yes, thank you.'

His mouth curved into a faint smile. 'So polite. More coffee?'

She shook her head, then watched as he gestured to the waiter to bring the bill.

'Shall we leave?' Michel queried minutes later, and Sandrine rose to her feet in acquiescence.

Together they strolled along the main street, pausing every now and then to examine a shop window display. Sandrine purchased a few postcards, added moisturiser and sun-screen cream, insisting on paying for them herself. Use of her credit card took care of a bikini and sarong wrap in glorious turquoise.

'The resort pool or the ocean?' Michel asked as they deposited an assortment of carry bags in their hotel suite.

She didn't hesitate for a second. 'Ocean.'

It took only minutes to change, collect a towel and cross the street to the beach.

A number of people inhabited the clean white sand; children laughed and squealed as they played while adults were bent on improving their tans or relaxing beneath large beach umbrellas.

The sea looked peaceful, with the gentle waves of an incoming tide encroaching on the foreshore. The curved bay was picturesque with its outcrop of rocks, a steep, bush-clad hill that led to a Natural Reserve.

There were many such beaches, coves and bays along the eastern coast, but Noosa held a reputation all its own.

Bliss, Sandrine silently reflected as she spread her towel beneath the beach umbrella Michel had erected. First, she'd sunbathe, then she'd swim.

Applying sun-screen cream was a sensible precaution, given the strength of the summer sun, and it took only minutes to cover her legs, arms and midriff.

'What do you think you're doing?' she demanded as Michel extracted the plastic bottle and squeezed a generous portion onto his cupped fingers.

'Applying cream to your back.'

Her mouth pursed at the amusement apparent as he

began smoothing the protective cream onto her shoulders.

He was thorough. A little too thorough, she decided as he ensured every centimetre of exposed skin was covered. He even went to the extent of loosening the clip of her bikini top, then refastening it. And his fingers caused havoc with her nervous system as they conducted a firm, circling massage across her back, over her waist and down to the line of her bikini briefs. Controlling her breathing became an effort, and she was grateful her expression was hidden behind dark glasses.

'Thanks.' Her voice was husky, almost indistinct.

'You can return the favour,' Michel instructed her indolently, handing her the bottle.

His request was deliberate, she was sure of it. Part of a strategy to test the effect such an action would have on her. Well, she'd show him just how easy it was to touch him. It wouldn't trouble her at all.

Ten seconds in and she knew she lied. He could have done the macho thing and flexed every muscle. Instead, he simply sat with his knees raised, his back to her, and his breathing didn't alter a fraction as she completed the application in record time.

Sandrine didn't want to think about the way her pulse raced into overdrive or how every nerve end uncurled in sensitive anticipation. An ache began deep inside, radiating from her central core until it encompassed her whole body.

'All done,' she managed evenly as she recapped the

bottle, mirroring his movements as he stretched out, face down, on the towel.

Twenty minutes later she strode across the sand to the water's edge, took a few steps, then dived into the cool blue-green sea, emerging to the surface to cleave the waves with leisurely strokes parallel to the shore.

There was something infinitely tranquil about the unlimited expanse of an ocean and the sensation of being at one with nature. Quite different from using a swimming pool, she mused as she trod water and admired the exotic landscape with its many brightly painted, low-rise apartment buildings and houses dotting the foreshore.

It was—how long since she'd last holidayed in Noosa? Years, she perceived wryly. A midyear school break with her parents in the days before divorce had torn the family in two, introduced bitterness and a division of loyalties with the advent of step-parents and step-siblings.

Exclusive boarding schools had effectively ensured a safe haven when she no longer fitted easily into one family or the other. There had always been love and welcome whenever she visited. But there had also been an awareness she was a reminder of another life, another time. An awkwardness, she reflected, that had resulted from her own sensitivity. Something that could have had a detrimental effect.

Instead, she had learnt to be self-sufficient, to strive and succeed on her own merits. And she had, utilising her talent with speech and drama by channelling it into acting, initially in school plays. Part-time modelling with an agency resulted in her appearance in a television commercial, and the rest, as they say, became the substance of dreams when she was offered a character role in a long-running Australian television series.

A modelling assignment in New York during a seasonal filming hiatus had garnered an invitation to a party where Michel numbered one of several guests. Two linked events that had changed her life.

'Intent on solitude?'

Sandrine's eyes widened at the sound of that familiar drawl, and she turned to see Michel within touching distance. Wet hair and water streaking his face did nothing to detract from the chiselled perfection of his features or lessen the degree of power he managed to exude without any effort at all.

'No.'

'Care to try your hand at something more adventurous?'

She was unable to read anything from his expression, and his eyes were too intently watchful for her peace of mind. 'Such as?'

'Hang-gliding, parasailing, jet-skiing?'

'Surely you jest?'

'Hiring a boat and exploring the waterways?' Michel continued as if she hadn't spoken, and she scooped up a handful of water and splashed him with it. 'I could retaliate,' he warned.

'I'm trembling.'

His lips formed a musing smile. 'It can wait.'

It wasn't the words but the implication that sent a

shivery sensation feathering the surface of her skin. His eyes held a warm, purposeful gleam that did much to melt through a layer of her resolve.

Her eyes remaining locked with his, she was aware of him to a degree that was vaguely frightening. Magnetic sensuality. She didn't want to be held in its thrall, for it clouded logic and decimated any rationale.

Michel divined her ambivalence, successfully attributed its cause and chose to cut her a little slack. 'Race you in to shore.'

He even held back, matching his strokes to meet hers, and they emerged from the water together. On reaching their shaded location, he caught up his towel, blotted off the excess moisture, then wound and secured the towel low on his hips.

'Feel like a drink?'

'After a shower and I've changed into something a little more respectable,' Sandrine parried as she copied his actions.

Michel pulled the beach umbrella from the sand and returned it to the hire stand en route to their hotel. 'Go on up,' he directed when they reached the entrance. 'I'll be there in ten minutes.'

She inclined her head, then crossed to Reception to collect their room card. Inside their suite, she made straight for the shower and emerged into the bedroom to discover Michel in the process of discarding several glossy signature carry bags onto the bed.

'You've been shopping.'

'Something to wear to dinner,' he declared as he divided and emptied the bags. 'Here.' He picked up a tissue-wrapped package and tossed it onto the pillow. 'This is for you.'

This, she discovered, was a pair of black silk evening trousers, together with a silk camisole in soft antique gold. There was also a pair of exquisite, lacy black briefs.

'Thanks,' she murmured appreciatively, watching as he shook free a pair of black slacks and a deep blue, short-sleeved silk shirt.

If only he'd relayed his intention to stay overnight, she could have packed a few clothes and he'd have saved some money. Although money was hardly an issue, she decided as she discarded the towel and quickly donned underwear.

The evening trousers and camisole were a perfect fit, and she was in the process of applying make-up when Michel re-entered the room.

Sandrine glanced away from the mirror and met his gleaming gaze. 'They're lovely,' she complimented.

'*Merci*,' he acknowledged with mocking amusement as he discarded the towel.

She returned her attention to applying eye shadow, willing her fingers to be steady as she brushed a soft gold to one upper lid.

The mirror proved her worst enemy, for it reflected heavily muscled thighs, smooth hips and buttocks and a fleeting glimpse of male genitalia as he stepped into briefs. The action involved in pulling on the pair of dark trousers emphasised an impressive display of honed muscle and sinew, and she was unable to glance away as he shrugged into his shirt and tended to the buttons.

Get over it, she derided in silent chastisement, and determinedly focused her attention on completing her make-up. It was something of a relief to enter the en suite minutes later, and she activated the hair dryer, opting to leave her hair to fall loose onto her shoulders.

'Beautiful,' Michel complimented when she re-entered the bedroom. 'But there's something missing.'

She felt on edge, jittery in a way that could only be attributed to acute sensitivity to this particular man. All her fine body hairs seemed to stand on end, quivering like miniature antennae, and her stomach didn't belong to her at all.

This was madness. Why did she feel as if she were being stalked by a prowling predator waiting for the right moment to pounce?

'What is that?' she managed lightly, and felt her body tremble slightly as he moved towards her.

'These.' He took hold of her left hand and slid first her wedding ring, then the magnificent pear-shaped diamond onto the appropriate finger.

Sandrine looked down at her hand, saw the symbols of his possession and didn't know whether to laugh or cry. 'Michel—'

Anything further she might have uttered was stilled as he pressed a finger to her lips. 'Let's go have that drink, shall we?'

The hotel lounge held a mix of patrons, and Michel quirked an eyebrow when she insisted on orange juice.

'The need for a clear head?'

'Definitely!'

'Afraid, Sandrine?'

Of you? 'No,' she responded evenly. Her reaction to him was something different entirely.

His husky chuckle was almost her undoing, and she could have hit him when he raised his glass in a silent, mocking gesture.

'How is your grandmother?' A safe subject, surely, she considered as she took a sip of the refreshing juice.

Michel's eyes held hers as he settled back in his chair. 'She expressed regret that you were unable to join me.'

Not so safe, she mentally corrected. 'She's an incredible lady.'

'Who regards you with affection.'

What could she say to that? After a few seconds she settled with 'How kind.'

'I promised we'd visit her after our return to New York.'

She didn't want to think that far ahead. It was enough just to get through each day.

'Would you like another drink?'

Sandrine shook her head, then watched as he set his empty glass down on the table. 'Shall we go have dinner?'

They chose Italian, the best restaurant, they were assured, in town. Michel ordered a smooth vintage Lambrusco to accompany a gnocchi starter, and they both settled for veal scallopini as a main, with an exquisite lemon tart for dessert.

The ambience was definitely European, the waiters

were Italian, and the food...*perfetto*. Sandrine expressed her pleasure as the waiter served them with a liqueur coffee.

'I don't think I'll eat a thing until at least midday tomorrow,' she declared as they walked out onto the street.

One shoestring strap slipped down over her shoulder and she absently slid it back in place. It had been a great few hours, reminding her far too vividly of previous evenings they'd shared over good food and fine wine.

'That was nice,' she said, offering him a warm smile. 'Thank you.'

His expression was equally warm, and those brilliant grey eyes bore a gleam she didn't care to define. 'My pleasure.'

'Let's walk,' she suggested on impulse. Hastings Street ran parallel to the foreshore, and it wasn't late. A number of tourists were enjoying the evening air, walking, drinking coffee at pavement tables adjoining numerous cafés and restaurants.

Michel caught her hand loosely in his, and she didn't pull free.

Did they look like lovers? Somehow she didn't think so. Their body language wasn't right.

He traced an idle pattern across the delicate veins at her wrist and felt the sudden surge in her pulse as it leapt to a faster beat.

When she attempted to tug her hand free, he forestalled the action by lifting her hand to his lips and kissing each finger in turn, aware of the slight tremor that shook her slender frame.

Sandrine lifted her head and met his steady gaze. 'Are you trying to seduce me?'

'Am I succeeding?'

Only too well.

'Resorting to the neutrality of silence, *mignonne*?'

She offered him a stunning smile. 'Of course.'

'On the grounds that anything verbal might give me a swelled head?'

'Something like that.'

They strolled along one side of the street, pausing every now and then when something in a shop window caught their attention, then they crossed over and wandered back to their hotel.

It was after eleven when she preceded him into their suite, and she automatically stepped out of her shoes, then reached for the waistband of her evening trousers.

Only to discover he'd already beaten her to it. She stood perfectly still as he slid the garment down past her thighs and she didn't move when he slipped the camisole over her head.

It was difficult to retain much dignity clad only in lacy black briefs, and she retreated into the en suite as Michel began divesting his clothes.

The lack of a nightgown caused her a moment's consternation, then she plucked a towel free and wound it sarongwise round her slim form. She might have little option but to sleep nude, but she was darned if she'd walk naked into the bedroom!

Misplaced modesty, she decided ruefully as she met

the dark, gleaming gaze of the man settled comfortably against a nest of pillows. The expanse of sun-kissed olive skin covering honed muscle and sinew was impossible to ignore, so she didn't even try.

His faintly quirked brow didn't help any, nor did his slow, teasing smile as she slid between the sheets before discarding the towel.

'It's a little late to play shy, *chérie*.'

'Perhaps I don't feel comfortable parading nude.'

'Do you?'

A slight frown creased her forehead. 'Do I—what?'

'Feel uncomfortable with me,' Michel pursued patiently as he rolled towards her and supported his head with a propped elbow.

He was too close, and much too dangerous. She became conscious of her breathing and monitoring every breath she took. The beat of her heart seemed loud in her chest, and she was willing to swear the pulse at the base of her throat was visible and far too fast.

'*I* feel uncomfortable with me when I'm around you,' Sandrine admitted with husky honesty, and her eyes widened as he lifted a hand and stroked a forefinger lightly down the length of her nose.

'And that's bad?' He pressed the pad of his thumb against her lower lip, then slowly traced its curve.

Heat suffused her body and pooled between the apex of her thighs. Sensation flared deep within, and her fingers clenched in an effort to control the aching need that made her want to reach for him.

'You're doing this deliberately, aren't you?' Sandrine queried in a slightly strangled voice.

'What am I doing, *mignonne*?'

'Seducing me.'

His head lowered and his lips brushed against her own. 'Mmm,' he teased, his breath warm as it mingled with her own. 'Want me to stop?'

She nearly said *yes*. Then his mouth was on hers, gentle at first, then the pressure increased as he took her deep.

Unbidden, her arms lifted as she linked hands at his nape, and she held on during the sensual storm that followed, giving, taking, in a manner that left her weak-willed and malleable. *His*.

It was a long time before they lay spent, and curled in each other's arms they drifted easily into a blissful sleep from which they stirred in the early dawn hours to shower, then make exquisitely slow love until the waiter delivered their breakfast.

'What to you want to do with the day?' Michel queried as he drank the last of his orange juice, then poured strong black coffee.

Sandrine spooned muesli and fruit, added milk into a bowl, then looked enviously at the plate of bacon, eggs and fried tomato. She was famished. And filled with a languid warmth that owed everything to sensual and sexual satiation.

'Maleny, Montville, the Glasshouse Mountains.'

'I was afraid you would suggest that.'

'Why?' she asked, feigning innocence. 'What else did you have in mind?'

'We could stay here, order a late lunch, then drive back to the Coast.'

The thought of spending several more hours in bed with him would weaken her defences, and they couldn't afford to be weakened further! 'It's a new day,' she proffered solemnly. 'Let's make good use of it.'

'My intention precisely.'

'Let's not go for overkill. We scratched an itch, and it was great.' Better than great. There weren't the words to even begin a satisfactory description for what they'd shared.

His gaze sharpened. 'That's all it was for you? Scratching an itch?'

Sandrine lifted her cup, sipped the dark, sweet brew, then replaced it on the saucer. 'You want to conduct an analysis, Michel? Should I determine a points system and rate you accordingly?'

He wanted to drag her to her feet, sweep her back into the bedroom and change that tepid warmth into blazing heat.

She'd been with him every inch of the way, through the night and in the morning. He was prepared to stake his life on it. He'd felt the tremors shake her body, the sweet tug of her muscles as she took and held him in a fit so snug he grew hard at the very thought of it.

She was slipping into self-protection mode in the clear light of day. He could cope with that as long as he had the nights.

'I don't recall your confiding too many comparisons,' he drawled. 'And as we never did indulge in the Was-it-as-good-for-you-as-it-was-for-me? scenario, I see no reason to begin now.'

'Confidence is a fine thing.'

'Knowledge,' Michel corrected with a tinge of mockery. 'Of you.'

Oh, yes, he had that, she admitted wryly. He knew precisely which buttons to push, and where and when. It gave him an unfair advantage.

They finished breakfast in silence, then showered and dressed before checking out of the resort and collecting the car.

It was a beautiful day, the sky a clear azure with only a few wispy clouds in sight. Warm sunshine promised high summer temperatures as they left Noosa and headed towards the mountains.

Soon there were roadside stalls selling a variety of fruit and vegetables, and as they ascended, the ground undulated with acre upon acre in a patchwork of green pasture. It was a visual vista Sandrine found relaxing.

Not so relaxing were the events of last night. It was all too easy to reflect on the heaven of being in Michel's arms, savouring his taste, his touch, exulting in the sheer sensation of two lovers in perfect accord.

Even now, her body ached in places, and all it took was one glance, a vivid memory, and the heat began to simmer deep inside, flaring acutely until Michel became her total focus. Intense sexual chemistry, and ruinous to her peace of mind.

It brought a lump to her throat for a few long seconds and made swallowing difficult.

Dear heaven, think of something else! There, in the

paddocks, were cattle, and overhead a helicopter swung east. On a rescue mission, perhaps?

The car braked suddenly and an arm shot out in front of her, providing a barrier as she was flung forward against her seat belt simultaneously with Michel's muffled oath.

'What on earth?' Sandrine queried in startled surprise as the car came to a screeching halt, only to see the answer for herself as a small dog streaked from the road into the opposite paddock.

'Idiot animal. It could have been killed,' Michel muttered angrily as he directed her an encompassing glance. 'Okay?' She nodded wordlessly, and his gaze sharpened. 'Sure?'

He caught hold of her chin between thumb and forefinger and turned her head towards him, subjecting her to a sweeping appraisal.

'Yes.' It would never do for him to guess her shaken composure was due to *him*, and not the near accident.

She lifted a hand to her throat to hide the fast-beating pulse thudding in the hollow there, and she breathed a silent sigh of relief when he released her and turned his attention back to the road.

It was almost midday when they reached Montville, and Sandrine was captivated by the quaint buildings, the cafés and tearooms, the abundance of craft shops.

Together they browsed in a few of the shops, and she selected a few gifts for her step-siblings, then they enjoyed a delicious lunch in a café overlooking the valley before heading back to the Gold Coast.

It had been a pleasant break, and she said so as they entered the Sanctuary Cove villa just after six.

'All of it?' Michel drawled with a distinctly wicked smile.

'Most of it,' Sandrine qualified, and heard his faint laugh.

'Let's change and eat out.'

'I could make something,' she prevaricated, mentally assessing the contents of the refrigerator. It held steak, sufficient greens to make a salad, and fresh fruit.

'I'll book a table at the Hyatt,' Michel determined firmly.

'I have lines to study,' Sandrine warned as he placed the heel of his hand at the back of her waist and propelled her towards the stairs.

'We'll be home by nine. You can curl up in a chair and go through them then.'

Sandrine chose a casually elegant cream pant suit, dressed it up with gold, stiletto-heeled sandals, then fixed a long, matching cream fringed scarf at her neck so that half its length trailed down her back.

The Hyatt was well patronised, and the maître d' escorted them to a table close to a window with a pleasant view out over the river.

Michel ordered wine, then they selected their starter and main course, but deferred dessert.

Sandrine was enjoying her prawn starter when she heard a familiar light voice exude an affectionate greeting, and there was Cait London, a veritable feminine siren dressed in black, looking like a model who'd just stepped out of *Vogue*, hair and make-up the picture of perfection. With Gregor at her side.

'*Darling*,' Cait effused, proffering an air kiss to one cheek. 'Fancy seeing you here.'

Sandrine spared Gregor a quick glance, glimpsed the slight roll of his eyes and deduced that Cait was on a mission. A mission named 'snaring Michel'.

'The long arm of coincidence,' Sandrine agreed, and sent Michel a mocking glance beneath partly veiled eyelashes.

'You won't mind if we join you?' Cait slipped into a chair without waiting for an answer.

Oh, *great*. This held the promise of turning into quite an evening.

'I'll order another bottle of wine,' Gregor insisted as the wine steward and the waiter hovered attentively while Cait and Gregor perused the menu and gave their order.

Cait turned towards Sandrine. 'Are you not feeling well, darling?' False concern coloured her voice, and Sandrine silently applauded Cait's acting ability. 'You look a little pale.'

Sandrine summoned a sweet smile. 'Do you think so?'

'Gregor is hosting a party Saturday night. You must both come.'

'Unfortunately we'll be in Sydney,' Michel drawled, and lifted his glass to take an appreciative sip.

Really? Sandrine queried silently. She certainly intended to visit her family there, but she hadn't given a thought to whether Michel would join her.

Cait hid her disappointment well. 'What a shame.'

The waiter removed their plates and returned in minutes with Cait's and Gregor's starters.

'It should be an interesting shoot tomorrow.' Sandrine could almost sense Cait's sharpening figurative claws as she sought to scratch. 'Sandrine has this intimate scene.' She paused, then went for the kill. 'Knowing she's with other men must be difficult for you to handle.'

'I don't have a problem with it.' Michel's smile was deadly, his voice dangerously soft. 'Considering I'm the one who gets to take her to bed.'

Sandrine watched with fascination as Cait fluttered her lashes. 'I adore a proprietorial male.'

'Really, darling?' Gregor interposed. 'You surprise me. I had you pegged as calling the shots in a relationship.'

If looks could kill, Gregor would be dead and Cait would be up on a murder charge, Sandrine mused.

Well versed in the subtle games some women felt compelled to play, on one level she found Cait's behaviour amusing. On another, she wanted to scratch her eyes out! Jealousy, she reflected wryly, was not an enviable trait.

She spared Michel a quick glance and caught the faint gleam evident in those grey eyes. Was she that transparent? He had acquired the ability to read her mind with remarkable accuracy almost from the be-

ginning, whereas his was mostly a closed book. As a
poker player, he would be superb.

The waiter appeared with Cait's and Gregor's main
dishes, and Sandrine concentrated on doing her salmon
justice.

'How long will you stay in Sydney?'

Sandrine had to hand it to Cait…she was persistent.
'I'm—' not sure, she was going to add, except Michel
intercepted.

'Until the film wraps up and the publicity is done.'

'And afterwards?' Cait persisted with light coquetry. Michel proffered a polite smile. 'New York.
Then Paris.' He turned towards Sandrine, caught hold
of her hand and lifted it to his lips.

Careful, Sandrine silently warned. This is definitely
overkill.

Except there was nothing she could do to still the
tide of warmth sweeping through her body. It was as
if his slightest touch activated a switch, leaving her
with little or no control over her emotions. Something
she found difficult to bear, given the state of their relationship.

'French is such a romantic language,' Cait said with
an envious sigh. 'To have a lover so lost to passion in
my arms he lapses into his native tongue…it drives
me wild.'

'There have been so many,' Gregor drawled. 'One
imagines you must be multilingual.'

'Beast.'

'Just telling the truth as I know it, darling.'

Cait transferred her attention to Sandrine. 'I've auditioned for the lead in a new Lucas film. I think I'll get it.' She smoothed a hand over her hair. 'Do you have anything in mind?'

Sandrine replaced her cutlery and sipped the contents of her glass. 'Congratulations.'

'You didn't answer my question.'

She was conscious of Michel's intent interest in her response and deliberated for several seconds. 'I don't have any immediate plans.'

'Coffee, *chérie*?' Michel queried smoothly, and he summoned the waiter as she shook her head. 'You'll excuse us if we leave.' He made it a statement. 'I need to check some computer data, and Sandrine has to study her lines.' He signed the credit slip, then rose to his feet. 'Good night.'

They reached the main entrance and within minutes the concierge had summoned their car. Sandrine slid into the passenger seat and laid her head against the cushioned rest.

'No comment?'

She turned her head slightly as Michel eased the car onto the bricked roadway and negotiated the roundabout. 'None whatsoever,' she offered wryly, and heard his low, husky laugh.

Within minutes Michel activated the security gate leading to the waterfront villas, and in no time at all he drew the car to a halt inside the garage.

'Where would you prefer to study?' he asked as they entered the lounge.

'Here.' She wanted to kick off her shoes and curl up in one of the cushioned chairs.

'I'll set my laptop up on the dining-room table.' He shrugged off his jacket and hooked it over one shoulder. 'Will you make coffee, or shall I?'

'You,' she delegated. 'I'm going upstairs to change.'

Michel was still bent over the laptop when she re-entered the bedroom a few minutes before midnight, and she fell asleep within minutes of her head hitting the pillow.

She didn't hear him slip into bed beside her, nor was she aware of his arm drawing her close.

CHAPTER SIX

SANDRINE breathed a sigh of relief. Seven takes wasn't bad. The scene had come together, no one had fluffed their lines, and the electric intensity had been achieved at a level even Tony could applaud.

She was tired, hot, and the boned corselet pulling her waist into an impossibly small measurement was killing her. The heavy make-up felt as if it was a mask of greasepaint about to slide off her face, and if she didn't get rid of the elaborately coiffed wig *soon*, she'd scream.

Added to which, it was late, and she was impossibly thirsty and hungry. The instant she discarded the heavy period costume, she intended to drink half a litre of water, follow it with a powdered protein drink, then sink her teeth into a fresh, crisp apple.

'You look fragile, darling,' Gregor murmured. 'Too many late nights catching up on time lost between the sheets?'

'Yes.' She was in no mood to participate in his game of verbal thrust and parry.

'Lucky you.'

She offered him a stunning smile. 'Aren't I just?'

'Our esteemed investor looks immensely *physical*. Tires you out, does he?'

'Wrong, Gregor,' she responded sweetly.

His eyes gleamed. 'Mmm, hidden talents, darling?'

She merely smiled and crossed to join the wardrobe assistant.

Twenty minutes later she felt considerably better, dressed in jeans and a T-shirt, her feet encased in heeled sandals, her hair twisted into a careless knot at her nape. All she had to do was check what time she had to report on the set the next day, then she was free to go home.

Seven was an improvement on the early hour of five, and she turned towards the exit, caught sight of Michel deep in conversation with a man whose tall frame seemed familiar.

Both men glanced up at the same time, and Sandrine's eyes widened in surprise at his identity. What on earth was Michel's elder brother doing here? She'd last seen Raoul Lanier three months ago in Paris. Then, he'd regarded her with warmth and affection.

Sandrine was aware of his veiled scrutiny as she crossed to where they stood.

'Finished for the day?' Michel queried.

'I was just checking tomorrow's filming schedule.' She turned towards the man at his side. 'Raoul,' she greeted evenly. 'How are you?'

'Well. And you?' he returned smoothly.

'Fine.' Such polite formality. Her smile was overbright. 'When did you arrive?'

'This morning.'

Ask a direct question and she might get a direct answer. 'A social visit?'

'Not entirely.'

'Raoul is joining me in meetings with marketing,' Michel informed her in a voice that held a faint sardonic edge. 'Then he's due in Sydney to initiate negotiations on another matter.'

'Taking care of business,' Sandrine mocked lightly, aware of Raoul's level scrutiny.

'Yes.'

'I didn't ask Michel to inject finance to rescue the film.'

'I'm aware of that.'

'You mean to ensure he's not making a foolish investment.' It was a statement, not a query.

'Michel makes his own decisions.'

'Obviously.'

Raoul's gaze didn't falter. 'I understand you've reconciled?'

'We're working on it,' Michel drawled.

'And you, Sandrine,' Raoul posed. 'Are you working on your marriage to my brother?'

'Michel is sharing my villa, and my bed.' She'd wanted to shock him, but there wasn't a flicker of emotion evident on those chiselled features.

'That doesn't answer my question.'

'It's as much as you're going to get.' She turned on her heel and walked away. One Lanier brother was enough. Two was one too many!

Sandrine was halfway to Sanctuary Cove when her mobile phone rang, and she automatically engaged it.

'Raoul is meeting Stephanie Sommers, the film's

marketing representative, for dinner,' Michel informed her. 'He has invited us to join them.'

'No.'

'I'll be home in an hour.'

'*No*, Michel.' The stressed negative went unheard for he'd already ended the call.

She depressed the button and tossed the phone onto the passenger seat. Damn him. She cursed him again as she garaged the car and ran lightly upstairs.

An hour later she had showered, dressed, and was applying the finishing touches to her make-up when Michel walked into the bedroom.

He gave her a long, considered look, then quirked one eyebrow. 'Dressed to do battle?'

Black did things for her. It highlighted the texture of her skin, accented the burnished sheen of her sable-coloured hair and emphasised her luminous brown eyes.

Sandrine capped the mascara wand and tossed it into her make-up bag. 'You could say that.' She turned towards him. 'What time and where is this momentous dinner taking place?'

'At the Mirage Hotel, in an hour.'

She tossed a lipstick into her evening purse and snapped it shut. 'It'll take twenty minutes to reach Main Beach.' She slid the long chain strap over one shoulder and walked to the door. 'I'll be in the lounge catching the evening news.'

She descended the stairs and moved into the lounge, switched on the television and prowled the room, too restless to sit.

Mindful that she'd eaten very little all day, she filled a glass with water and drank it, then she splashed a small quantity of excellent Chardonnay into a crystal goblet.

It was half an hour before Michel entered the lounge, and the sight of him adorned in black evening suit, crisp white shirt and dark tie made the breath catch in her throat.

He possessed an exigent sexual chemistry that melted her bones. Dear heaven. How was it possible to want something so badly with your heart, yet conversely deny it with the dictates of your brain?

With a faintly mocking gesture she lifted the goblet in a silent salute, then raised it to her lips and took a small sip. 'This is solely for Stephanie's benefit.'

'The wine, or your attendance at dinner?'

A slow smile curved her generous mouth. 'Dinner. It isn't fair to pitch her alone among the wolves.'

'*Wolves*, Sandrine?' he queried with ill-concealed mockery. 'Isn't that a little extreme?'

'No.'

His voice held a certain dryness. 'I'm sure Stephanie can take care of herself.'

'Against Raoul? Are you kidding?'

It would be interesting to see how Stephanie reacted to the elder Lanier brother. A single mother raising a child alone had to have more than her share of courage and perspicacity.

'I'm sure you'll enjoy playing the role of her protector,' Michel mused as he crossed the room.

With one hand he extracted the goblet from her fingers and placed it on a nearby side table. At the same time he slid his other hand to cup her nape, drawing her close as his mouth fastened over her own in a kiss that tore at the restraints of his control.

He felt a slight tremor slither through her slim frame and he deepened the kiss to something that resembled possession.

It was several minutes before he slowly lessened the intensity, trailing the soft, swollen curve of her lower lip with a touch as light as a butterfly's wing.

'We'd better leave or we'll be late,' Michel murmured as he eased her to arm's length.

Sandrine stood motionless for a few seconds, her eyes wide in a face that was pale beneath its cosmetic enhancement. Then she extracted a lip pencil from her evening purse and crossed to the ornate mirror to effect repairs to a mouth devoid of colour.

Her fingers shook slightly, and she cursed beneath her breath at the level of emotional helplessness Michel was able to achieve.

When she was done, she replaced the lip pencil in her purse and preceded him through to the garage, slipping into the passenger seat as he slid in behind the wheel.

The Sheraton Mirage resort was built on a narrow peninsula, a luxury low-rise facing the ocean. It was renowned for its innovative design, extensive use of marble, an elegant waterfall and tranquil views out over a wide pool with its island bar to the ocean beyond.

Michel relinquished the car to the valet to park, and

Sandrine entered the magnificent foyer at his side. Raoul rose to his feet from one of the large cushioned sofas and moved forward to meet them. Of Stephanie there was no sign.

'Punctuality appears not to be Ms Sommers's forte,' Raoul indicated dryly. 'Shall we go into the lounge for a drink while we wait?'

'Maybe she's caught up in traffic.'

'Or the baby-sitter didn't show or the child was sick,' Raoul added with thinly veiled mockery.

So he'd had Stephanie investigated. Undoubtedly initiated before he left Paris as part of the Lanier modus operandi, Sandrine concluded cynically.

'I imagine if Stephanie is going to be delayed for any length of time, she'll call,' she felt impelled to defend.

At that moment a cell phone rang, and Raoul extracted a slim compact model from inside his dinner jacket. Two minutes and two curt words later, he cut the connection.

'It appears Ms Sommers has been held up with a flat tyre. She'll be another ten minutes.'

Stephanie entered the lounge one minute ahead of time, and Sandrine had to admire her cool unruffled demeanour as she crossed to where they sat.

'I must apologise. I hope there wasn't a problem holding the booking?' She glanced from one man to the other and offered Sandrine a warm smile. 'Shall we go in?'

Sandrine silently applauded Stephanie's style. The

young marketing executive had panache. What's more, she wasn't averse to taking control.

Something Michel would soon alter in his favour, Sandrine perceived as the maître d' seated them at their table and beckoned the drinks waiter. To whom Stephanie made it clear *she* was hostess.

Michel's features were inscrutable, while Raoul opted for chilling politeness.

Perusing the menu and selecting a starter and main required deliberation, and when their orders were placed Michel eased back in his chair and regarded the attractive strawberry blonde seated opposite with studied ease.

'Perhaps you'd care to relay your marketing strategy, Ms Sommers.' He paused a beat. 'For this film in particular.'

'Stephanie,' the marketing executive corrected with a faint smile. 'When we receive the finished film from the studio, it will be viewed in a private cinema by about thirty people. We'll then arrange meetings to discuss the target market and determine to what age group the film will have most appeal.'

Sandrine watched as Stephanie paused to lift her glass and take a measured sip of chilled water. Her hand was steady, her actions carefully controlled, and she displayed admirable poise as she replaced the glass and subjected both men to a level gaze.

'Further discussions will follow on which segments should be selected for the trailer, the shots to appear in press releases overseas and locally, and which of these will be released to the television stations and other media, including the entertainment pages in newspapers and magazines.'

'Worldwide?' Michel queried, and Stephanie inclined her head in silent acquiescence.

'Of course,' she confirmed. 'We'll also push to heighten public awareness of the film by organising a fashion shoot with one of the prestige fashion magazines to ensure coverage in the major national weekly magazines.'

'In which only the lead actors appear?' Raoul posed.

'Not always,' Stephanie qualified, and Sandrine successfully hid a faint smile at the other woman's ability to cover all the angles. 'We can arrange to include focused shots of local actors to draw their attention to their involvement in the film. Press shots of Michel and Sandrine at a social gala would draw public attention and highlight the film.'

'Sandrine's involvement in professional modelling would also be of interest, would it not?'

The waiter arrived with their starters, and there was a pause as the wine steward made a production of opening a bottle of wine, which he mistakenly proffered to Raoul for tasting.

Sandrine watched with interest as Raoul deferred the sampling to Stephanie and she could only admire her very skilled acceptance. For a moment she even thought she caught a glimpse of amusement in Raoul's gaze, only to decide it was her imagination.

'We organise press interviews in the star's hotel,' Stephanie elaborated, 'or if they've stipulated private leasing, we arrange a mutually agreeable venue for the interview.'

'Simultaneously?'

'In an intense push to raise public awareness.'

'Impressive,' Michel commented, and began on his starter.

'It's my job to impress.'

'Tell me,' Raoul interjected in a deceptive drawl. 'Don't you have family obligations that might interfere with total dedication to optimum marketing of this film?'

Sandrine wanted to kick his shin *hard* beneath the table. What game was he playing, for heaven's sake?

'I'm sure you're already aware I'm a single mother with a three-year-old daughter,' Stephanie responded smoothly. 'Should there be a crisis, I'd deal with it in the best way possible.' She fixed Raoul with a penetrating look. 'And my daughter would always take precedence.' Her chin lifted fractionally. 'Does that answer your question?'

Oh, my, Sandrine breathed. It was possible to cut the air with a knife!

'Yes.'

'Good.'

Michel cast his brother a brief, considering glance, then returned his attention to his starter.

'Were you able to get a baby-sitter for tonight without difficulty?' Sandrine posed conversationally.

'Given that I had very short notice, yes.'

'The Lanier brothers expect instant action in response to their slightest whim.' She was conscious of Michel's swift glance but ignored it.

'Really?' Stephanie's voice was dry. 'And you married one of them?'

'I thought it was a good idea at the time.'

'Total bewitchment, followed by a reality check?'

'Something like that,' Sandrine said with a wicked smile. She was beginning to enjoy herself!

'More wine, Ms Sommers?' Raoul queried silkily.

'Stephanie,' the marketing executive corrected with equal smoothness. 'And no, thank you. I get to drive home after this.'

'Pity.'

'For declining the wine?'

Sandrine watched as Raoul leant back in his chair. She seriously doubted any woman of his acquaintance had challenged him on any count.

'For endeavouring to treat this as other than a business meeting.'

'That's unfair,' Sandrine protested quickly.

'And unjustified,' Stephanie added, folding her napkin and placing it beside her plate. 'You insisted on meeting tonight.' She picked up her evening purse and focused her attention on Michel. 'I've already relayed our marketing strategy. Therefore my presence here is no longer necessary. Enjoy the rest of your meal.'

Sandrine watched the attractive blonde turn from the table and step quickly towards the main desk, pause briefly as she presented a credit card, then disappear through the door.

'A slight case of overkill, Raoul?' Michel mocked,

raising one eyebrow at his brother's narrowed gaze, then added thoughtfully, 'Are you going to let her get away?'

Raoul shifted his napkin onto the table and rose to his feet. 'No, I don't believe I am.'

'That was extremely—'

'Inappropriate,' Michel completed with dry cynicism.

'Yes, it was.'

'I hope he catches her.'

'Even if he does, I doubt it'll do him any good,' Sandrine opined, annoyed at Raoul's inexplicable behaviour and Michel's subsequent amusement.

'You don't think Raoul will be able to mend fences?' He lifted his glass and took an appreciative sip of the excellent wine.

'Not easily.'

His eyes gleamed with humour as they swept her expressive features. 'You don't think my brother would benefit from the love of a good woman?'

'Whatever happened to the reverse side of the coin?' Sandrine parried. 'Shouldn't a woman benefit from the love of a good man?'

'Of course.'

'It's unfortunate the Lanier men have their thinking locked into another century.'

Michel's gaze narrowed fractionally. 'Specifically?'

The waiter removed their plates and summoned the wine steward to replenish their glasses.

'You're amused by Raoul's reaction to Stephanie. What if it progressed into something serious?' She lifted a hand in an expressive gesture. 'Do you imagine Raoul would countenance Stephanie's continuing with her career?'

He subjected her to an unwavering appraisal as he leant back in his chair with indolent ease. 'As you are determined to do?' he riposted with deceptive mildness.

'You don't get it, do you?'

'Get what, precisely?'

'It's not about a *career* as such.' She should have a script, dammit! She'd carefully thought out everything she wanted to say. Hell, she'd had enough time! Where were all those fine words now? Out the window, along with her sanity.

She took a slow, calming breath. 'It's about seizing an opportunity and striving to achieve the best possible result. Not for fame and fortune, but to satisfy a creative need.' She waited a few seconds before adding, 'Because there's a depth, an inner feeling so in tune with the part that you feel *you* are meant to be the medium to convey the written words, actions and emotions on film for the audiences to appreciate the true depth of the character.'

Michel remained silent. The silence stretched into minutes as the waiter brought their main course and made a production out of flourishing a gigantic pepper-mill, explaining the intricacies of the chef's skill before bidding them *bon appétit* in appalling French.

Michel picked up his fork and speared an artistically carved carrot rosette. 'You didn't pause to consider that if you got the part, it would involve your being

in Australia at a time when I was locked into important
business meetings in Paris?'

'Do you know how many actresses auditioned for
that part?' she demanded. 'My chances of succeeding
were as hopeful as a snowflake surviving in hell.'

He was calm, his movements controlled, but she
sensed leashed anger beneath the surface. 'Yet you did
succeed,' he reminded her with deceptive mildness.
'You also signed a contract, confirmed flight arrangements and waited to tell me coincidentally two days
prior to my being due in Paris.'

He pressed his fork into a baby potato, slid it into
the small pool of hollandaise sauce and sampled it
with evident enjoyment, then he lifted his head and
his gaze pierced hers, steady and unblinking. 'You expected me to say, ''That's fine, darling. Call me. See
you next month.''?'

The nerves in her stomach tightened and curled into
a painful knot. 'The timing was wrong. So was the
film location.' She ran the tip of a fingernail along the
hemmed edge of her napkin. 'I knew you'd protest,
but I hoped you'd understand.'

'Enough to agree to your being apart from me for
a considerable length of time?'

'It was only a few weeks.'

'At a time when I couldn't delegate in order to join
you,' he reminded her. 'If you remember, we opted
against an open relationship for the commitment and
permanency of marriage, determining to arrange our
lives so we could be together.'

'Are you implying I placed more importance on an acting part than *you*?'

'Deny your actions confirmed it.'

'You reacted as if I were a *possession*, someone who should be available whenever you happened to snap your fingers!' Sandrine accused, and saw his eyebrow lift in silent mockery. 'I wasn't referring to the bedroom!'

'I'm relieved to hear it,' Michel drawled.

'Am I interrupting something?'

Sandrine turned towards the owner of the faintly accented voice and summoned a wry smile. 'Only a current battle in the continuing war.'

Raoul slid into his seat. 'Want me to play mediator?'

'No,' she responded sweetly.

'Michel?'

'It'll keep.'

A devilish imp prompted the words that slipped easily from her tongue. 'We have a capricious airhead opposing a dictatorial tyrant.'

'A moment ago I was labelled possessive,' Michel relayed with marked cynicism, flicking his brother a dark glance. 'You caught up with Stephanie?'

'Yes.'

'I assume you offered an apology.'

'Which she refused to accept,' Raoul indicated dryly, and Sandrine proffered a musing grin.

'Verbally flayed you, did she?'

'You could say that.'

'So, when do you intend seeing her again?' Michel asked archly.

'Not at all, if she has anything to do with it.'

'Let me guess,' Sandrine posed. 'Tomorrow? On what grounds?'

Raoul lifted one eyebrow. 'Do I require any?'

No, of course he didn't, she dismissed. All he had to do was exert a measure of innate charm and women fell at his feet. Stephanie, she perceived, could prove to be an exception.

The waiter came with his main course and appeared affronted when Raoul dismissed his spiel before he even had the chance to begin with it.

'How long will it take to wrap up filming?' Raoul queried as he sliced into a succulent fillet of beef.

'I have another day scheduled. Maybe two at the most,' Sandrine told him. 'Tony is hopeful two weeks will do it.'

'I understand you have to remain on call for the possibility of retakes, publicity, promotion?'

'Yes.'

Raoul turned towards Michel. 'You intend remaining on the Coast?'

'Sydney,' Sandrine interjected. 'I have family there. If the studio calls me in, I can take the next flight out and be here the next day.'

'Aren't you forgetting something, *chérie*?' Michel queried silkily.

'You?' Her smile was a little too wide and too bright.

'So brave,' he mocked lightly.

Foolish, she amended silently, for thinking she could best him. Verbally, physically, or mentally.

'Dessert?'

'Coffee,' she said firmly, aware of the need to be decisive. 'Liqueur. Kahlua.'

Michel beckoned the waiter, conferred with Raoul, indicated their order, then requested the bill.

'The account has been settled, *m'sieur*.'

'I think you're mistaken.'

'No, *m'sieur*. The lady who was dining with you instructed the account be billed to her credit card.'

Sandrine hid a smile. Stephanie had managed to score on two counts. She'd walked out on Raoul Lanier and she'd added insult to injury by taking care of the bill.

'It appears Ms Sommers is a young woman to be reckoned with,' Michel commented dryly.

'Indeed.'

She detected mockery in Raoul's drawled response and was unable to suppress a grin. 'I'm with Stephanie.'

Both men sent her a level glance.

'Take her home,' Raoul instructed as he rose to his feet. 'And hush her mouth.'

Michel's eyes gleamed with humour. 'I intend to,' he said, suppressing a laugh.

Raoul accompanied them through the foyer to the main entrance and stood while the concierge summoned their car.

'Sweet dreams,' Sandrine teased as she bade Raoul goodnight, then slid into the passenger seat.

His expression was unreadable, and she gave a soft chuckle as Michel eased the car down to street level. Unless she was mistaken, Raoul had met his match, and she, for one, was going to enjoy watching the game!

The reception was uneventful, and the crowd thinned...

CHAPTER SEVEN

SANDRINE focused her attention on the scene beyond the windscreen as the car entered the flow of north-bound traffic.

The night was clear, the air sharp, and the lighted windows of various high-rise apartment buildings vied with far distant stars in an indigo sky.

'Shall we continue where we left off?'

She cast Michel a steady glance, aware that the night's shadows were highlighting the angles and planes of his face.

Her voice assumed unaccustomed cynicism. 'It won't change the fact that we had a major fight over my decision to fulfil an acting contract.'

He smote a clenched fist against the steering wheel, and she looked at him in startled disbelief.

'*Mon Dieu*. This is not about you pursuing a career.' He paused at a roundabout, waiting for two cars to circle and exit. 'It's about us being together. Not me being forced to spend time in one city while you're on the other side of the world in another. *Comprends*?'

'It was unavoidable.'

'It need not have been if you'd enlightened me about the audition at the time,' Michel enunciated with restraint. 'Thus giving me the opportunity to implement a contingency plan.' He directed her a dark look that spoke volumes before returning his attention to the road. 'I won't allow it to happen again.'

She drew in a deep breath and released it slowly. 'Excuse me? You won't *allow* it?'

'No,' he reiterated hardily. 'In future there will be no misunderstandings, no assumptions. We communicate and leave nothing in doubt.'

'I'm not sure we have a future,' she countered wretchedly, and could have bitten her tongue for uttering the foolish words.

'Oh, yes, we do, *mignonne*.' His voice was deadly soft.

'How can you say that?'

'Easily.'

'What about unresolved issues?'

'Name them,' Michel challenged.

'*You*,' Sandrine began, crossing each of his sins off on her fingers. 'Keeping tabs on me, investigating everyone to do with the film, conspiring to come up with a financial rescue package and making *me* a condition. Blackmail,' she asserted finally, 'is a criminal offense.'

'You're the wife of a wealthy man whose access to a family fortune makes anyone associated with me a prime target. Ransom, extortion, kidnapping. Of course I had someone watch over you.'

'You could have told me! How do you think I'd have reacted if I saw someone following me?'

'You refused to take or answer any of my calls, remember?' he retorted. 'And I pay for the best. Not some amateur who'd frighten you by being visible.'

'What did he do?' she demanded, immeasurably

hurt. 'Report whom I spoke to, where I went, what I did…every minute of every day?'

'It wasn't about my lack of trust in you,' he bit out angrily. 'It was about protection. *Yours*.'

'It was an invasion of privacy. *Mine*.' She was on a roll and couldn't seem to stop. 'I hate you for it.'

'So hate me, *mignonne*. At least I knew you were safe.'

'I guess the film running overtime and over budget played right into your hands. It gave you a lever, a figurative gun to hold to my head. *Do what I say, or else*.' She directed him a fulminating glare. 'I'll never forgive you for that.'

'"Never" is a long time.'

'It's as long as my lifetime.'

'Tell me,' Michel drawled. 'What did you intend to do when filming was completed?'

'Visit my family.'

'And afterwards?'

That was in the hazy future and something she'd deliberately not given much thought.

'I don't know,' she admitted honestly, and grimaced at the husky oath that rent the air.

'*You don't know*.' He raised both hands off the wheel, then gripped it hard. 'Next you'll tell me you intended contacting me through a lawyer.'

'I suppose it was a possibility.'

'Not telephoned me? Or caught a flight home?'

'Where *is* home, Michel?' she queried wryly. 'You have a residential base in several cities. I'd have had to have your secretary check on your whereabouts at the time.'

'*Sacré bleu.* You have my personal cell phone number where you can reach me anywhere at any time!'

'Maybe I wouldn't have wanted to!'

'Did it not occur to you that I might have taken all that into consideration and put, as you so cynically called it, "a figurative gun" to your head?'

The car slowed almost to a halt, and Sandrine was startled to see Michel activate the security gate permitting access to the Sanctuary Cove residential suburb. Seconds later the gate slid open and they drove through.

'Believe me, I would have used any weapon I had.'

'Blackmail, Michel?'

'You wouldn't answer my calls. If I arrived on your doorstep, would you have let me in?'

'Probably not.' At least, not at first. Her initial instinct would have been to slam the door in his face. The next...call the police? No, she refuted silently. She wouldn't have gone that far.

Was he right insisting on an enforced reconciliation? Putting them in the same residence, giving her no choice in the matter?

Within minutes they reached the villa, and once inside she crossed to the stairs and made her way up to the main bedroom.

For weeks she'd been so angry with Michel, herself, the circumstances that had caused the dissent between them. Now there was a degree of self-doubt, a measure of regret...and pain.

In the bedroom she slipped off her shoes and crossed to the floor-to-ceiling window. She made no attempt to draw the drapes as she looked out across the bay to the brightly lit restaurant cantilevered over the water.

Within a few days she'd leave here and probably not return. Sydney beckoned, and family. Her mother would be pleased to see her, likewise her father. But on separate occasions at different venues. She'd visit, take gifts, greet each of her step-siblings, and pretend she belonged.

She closed her eyes and tried to ignore the loneliness deep inside. An ache behind her eyelids culminated in tears that escaped and slid slowly down each cheek.

A faint sound, a slight movement, alerted her to Michel's presence, and she prayed he wouldn't turn on the light.

Sandrine sensed rather than heard him cross to stand behind her, then his hands closed over her shoulders as he drew her back against him.

'We made a deal, remember?'

'What deal are you referring to?'

'Never to spend a night apart. Except in circumstances beyond our control.'

So they had. And somehow taking a bit part in a movie being shot on the other side of the world didn't come close in the qualifying stakes of circumstances beyond our control.

'Where do we go from here?' she queried quietly, and he didn't pretend to misunderstand.

'Let's just take it one day at a time, hmm?'

For several minutes he didn't move, then his hands slid down her arms and linked together at her waist. She felt his lips brush against her ear, then trail slowly down the sensitive cord of her neck to nuzzle the soft hollow there.

It was heaven to lean her head into the curve of his shoulder and just *be*. To absorb the warmth of that large pulsing body, to take comfort in the shelter it afforded her, and to luxuriate in the touch of his hands, his lips.

He didn't offer a word, nor did she. They didn't move, just stood there for what seemed an age.

Then Michel gently turned her to face him, and she lifted her arms to encircle his neck as he lowered his head down to hers.

His mouth explored the soft lower curve of her own, grazing it with the edge of his teeth before sweeping his tongue to test the delicate tissues and tease the sensitised ridges in an erotic tasting that made her want more than this gentle supplication.

He'd removed his jacket and tie, but his shirt was an impossible barrier she sought to remove. She needed to touch his skin, to feel the heavy pulse of his heart beneath his rib cage and to explore the very essence of him.

By tacit agreement, they divested each other's clothes in a leisurely, evocative fashion, the slither of silk over skin arousing and heightening the senses to fever pitch.

Now. She wanted him *now*. Hard and fast. She needed to feel his strength, his unfettered passion.

Her mouth met his hungrily as he tumbled her down onto the bed, and she was aware of uttering small sounds of encouragement as he explored her, then she groaned out loud with pleasure as he entered her in one long thrust, stilling for timeless seconds as she absorbed him.

He withdrew and she lifted her hips as he plunged deep inside. She clung to him, urging him harder, closer, until pleasurable sensation reached an almost unbearable intensity.

Sandrine cried out, beseeching him with a litany of pleas as she became helpless beneath an emotion so treacherous it almost succeeded in destroying her.

Afterwards she could only lie there and attempt to regain control of her ragged breathing. And her sanity.

His eyes never left hers, and she felt as if she were drowning as he traced a finger over the soft curve of her mouth, probing the inner skin with erotic sensitivity.

Not content, he trailed a path down the length of her throat, then lowered his head to her mouth to create fresh havoc with her senses as he kissed her, thoroughly, mindlessly, then feathered his lips to the sensitive hollows beneath her throat, her breasts, savouring each peak in turn with devastating eroticism.

As he travelled lower, her body quivered, then tautened against an invasion so blatantly intimate she began to burn with the intoxicating heat of his touch.

After play merged into foreplay as passion reignited, and she was driven by a hunger so intense she became a willing wanton in his arms, taking intimate liberties that had him groaning beneath her as they both became lost in mesmeric rapture.

They took the late-morning flight out of Coolangatta airport, approaching the outskirts of Sydney just over an hour later.

The jet banked towards the ocean, providing a panoramic view of the harbour and city. Tall skyscrapers vied with elegant homes dotting numerous coves and inlets. Scenic landmarks such as the Sydney Harbour Bridge and the Opera House were distinctive from this height, and Sandrine felt the familiarity of home as they began their descent.

This was where she'd been born, raised and educated. Her family, her friends were here. For a while she could relax, visit family, meet friends and indulge a penchant for shopping.

The benefit of travelling first class was the speed of disembarking, and in no time at all Michel had collected their bags from the luggage carousel and organised a taxi.

It was a bright sunny day, with hardly a cloud in the sky. In some ways it seemed an age since she'd left Sydney; in others it was as if it were only yesterday.

Nothing had changed, she noted as the taxi took the customary route from the airport. Industrial areas gave way to semi-industrial, then residential. The terrace houses looked the same, although a few had received a fresh coat of paint. Traffic hurtled along the busy road at maximum speed, accompanied by the hydraulic hiss of heavily laden trucks, the occasional squeal of hastily applied brakes as a driver attempted a risky switch of lanes and miscalculated.

A turn-off led towards wide, tree-leafed roads, older-style homes, most lovingly restored and some still standing in palatial grounds.

Double Bay housed an eclectic mix of homes and apartment buildings. It was an inner suburb where old-money status sat next to new, where Porsches, Bentleys and BMWs parked nose to tail with Ferraris, Audis and Rolls-Royces. It housed one of the city's most exclusive shopping centres where trendy cafés nestled between designer boutiques, classy restaurants and a ritzy hotel.

Michel's apartment was situated atop a three-level, spacious old home that had been gutted and architecturally designed to resemble the original homestead. Pale lemon stucco with a white trim and black-painted, iron-lace railings provided a gracious exterior. Each floor housed a separate apartment, reached by a lift instead of the original staircase, and modern materials had been crafted to resemble the old, thereby retaining a sense of timeless grandeur that was complemented by exquisite antique furniture.

Sandrine had fallen in love with it at first sight, and now she crossed the spacious lounge to wide glass doors guarding the entrance to a long veranda that offered panoramic views over Port Jackson Harbour.

'Penny for them,' Michel teased with measured indolence as he joined her. He linked his arms around her waist and drew her back against him.

'Nothing in particular,' she said reflectively. 'Just a feeling of satisfaction at being home again.'

'You'll want to ring your family and make arrangements to meet them.'

'Yes,' she agreed. But not collectively. There was definitely a *yours* and *mine* definition apparent, and she'd learnt from an early age not to shift the line between the two!

'Lunch or dinner, whatever suits,' Michel offered. 'As long as I can put in a few hours on the laptop each day.'

She watched a ferry glide across the harbour and glimpsed a freighter on the horizon. 'You want to work this afternoon?'

'Unless you have a better idea.'

The temptation to tease him was irresistible. 'Well, it's ages since I had a manicure, my hair could do with a trim, and I need to replenish some make-up.'

'I work, you shop,' he quipped with a musing drawl.

'Are you sure you don't mind?'

His hands slipped up to cover her breasts, the touch light, tantalising, and she caught her breath at the sensual promise evident as his lips settled in the sensitive curve of her neck.

'Go, *chérie*. Be back by six, and we'll eat out.'

Unpacking could wait until later, and with a light laugh she slipped from his arms, caught up her shoulder-bag, then blew him a cheeky kiss before heading for the front door.

Sandrine enjoyed a wonderful few hours. The manicure proved to be no problem, and the hair salon readily fitted her in between appointments. Tempted by a trendy café, she ordered a cappuccino, a salad and sandwich, then she browsed among several boutiques lining a narrow street of converted old-fashioned cottages.

An arcade in the Ritz-Carlton Hotel housed several exclusive shops, and in one she discovered a perfect pair of shoes.

It was almost six when the taxi pulled into the kerb adjacent to the apartment, and she cleared security, then rode the lift to the top floor.

Michel was seated at an antique desk in one corner of the lounge, and he glanced up from the laptop as she entered the room. He'd changed out of his suit and wore dark chinos and an ivory chambray shirt.

He caught sight of the brightly coloured carry bags, glimpsed the beautifully styled hair and offered her a warm smile as he closed down the computer.

Sandrine deposited the bags on a nearby chair. 'I bought shoes.' She wrinkled her nose at him. 'Very expensive shoes.'

A husky laugh escaped his throat as he crossed to her side. 'Hmm, new perfume?'

'You noticed.'

'I notice everything about you.'

Just as she'd developed a keen sixth sense about him. The clean male smell of his soap and cologne, freshly laundered clothes and a masculine scent that was his alone.

'What time did you book the restaurant?'

'Seven.'

'Then I'd better go unpack, shower and dress.'

He slid a hand beneath her hair and cupped her nape as he lowered his head down to hers. The kiss held passion and promise, and she felt vaguely regretful as he let her go.

It was a warm summer's evening, and she selected black silk evening trousers, a jewelled singlet top, then added a sheer black evening blouse. Stiletto-heeled pumps, a matching jewelled evening bag completed the outfit. Make-up was understated, with emphasis on her eyes.

Michel had chosen a restaurant specialising in seafood, and they each selected a prawn starter and ordered grilled fish to follow. The wine steward presented a bottle of Dom Pérignon champagne.

'Did you get in touch with your parents?'

She felt guilty that she hadn't. 'I'll ring them both in the morning.'

He lifted his flute and placed the rim against her own. '*Salut.*'

Their starter arrived, and she bit into a succulent prawn and savoured the taste. Heaven. The sauce was perfect.

'With both you and Raoul in Australia, who is minding—'

'The store?'

'Figuratively speaking.'

'Henri heads a very capable team in our absence.'

'When is Raoul returning to Paris?'

His smile held a faint wryness. 'Twenty questions, Sandrine?'

She gave a slight shrug. 'Curiosity, I guess.'

'His plans are less flexible than mine.'

'And you, Michel?' she queried fearlessly. 'How long will you stay in Australia?'

His gaze was direct, unwavering. 'As long as it takes.'

She didn't pretend to misunderstand. Something curled inside her stomach and tightened into a painful ball. 'I might be called back to the Gold Coast studios to reshoot a scene. Then there's the publicity promotion…'

'I've been working, myself, every day since I arrived in Australia.'

The laptop. In this electronic age it was possible to access and transmit data at the touch of a button.

'It isn't necessary for—'

'Yes,' Michel interrupted. 'It is.'

The waiter removed their plates, and the wine steward refilled their flutes with champagne.

'Michel…' She trailed to a halt, and although her eyes searched his, she was unable to gain much from his expression.

'We promised to take each day as it comes, remember?'

Yes, so they had. But with every day that passed she realised how hard it would be to have to live without him. And she knew she didn't want to. It should be so simple to mend an emotional bridge. You just said the words, and everything was fixed.

Except they had to be the right words, and it had to be the right time and the right place.

When they made love, she freely gave him her body, her soul, and prayed he knew what he meant to her. But she was a wordless lover, and "I love you" hadn't passed her lips since the night before she left New York.

The waiter presented their main dish, and Sandrine looked at the succulent barramundi, the artistically arranged salad and discovered her appetite had fled.

So, too, had her conversational skills. For how did

you talk banalities with someone you'd soon share sexual intimacy?

She had only to look at him, and in her mind she could feel the touch of his hands, his lips, *know* the reaction of her traitorous body as he led her towards sensual fulfilment. Just as she knew *he* was equally as aware.

It was akin to a silent game they played. Except there was no deliberation, no premeditation. Intense sensual chemistry sizzled between them, ready to ignite as easily as dry tinder at the toss of a lighted match.

It had always been the same. Had she confused sexual attraction with love? *And what is love?*

If you took away sexual desire, what was left? A solid friendship? She would have said yes, until he forbade her to take the movie role. A friend would have been pleased she'd auditioned successfully.

Still, although friendship was important in marriage, a legal union was about commitment, honesty and trust. Because if you love, you want to commit, and there needed to be trust and honesty for the union to succeed.

When it came to honesty, she'd shifted the boundaries, signed a contract without his knowledge and against his wishes, confronted him at the eleventh hour, taken the flight, the job, regardless.

At the time she'd been so angry over his inflexibility she hadn't really given anything else coherent thought. There was a part of her that cherished the sanctity of marriage. And her feelings for Michel weren't in question.

Yet she was an independent young woman. She'd

owned her own apartment, her own car; she had not one, but two great jobs she loved, and for the past seven years she'd been a free spirit, answerable only to herself.

Why had she imagined marriage to Michel wouldn't change that?

Be honest, a small voice taunted. *Love* was the prime moving force in this union. She'd been so caught up in the wonder and magic of it all that she hadn't focused too much on the future.

Carpe diem. Seize the day. And she had, only too willing to allow Michel to sweep her off her feet, exultant with joy at the thought of sharing her life with this man, and confident love would conquer all.

In a world where women had fought and won equality with men in the business arena, she'd taken it for granted she would combine her career with marriage. Michel hadn't objected to her participating in a few modelling assignments. Why should he object to her taking a part in a film?

Yet he had. Warning irrevocably that he didn't view marriage as two partners pursuing separate careers and leading separate lives.

'The fish isn't to your liking?'

Sandrine glanced up quickly. 'No. I mean, yes.' She gave a helpless shrug. 'I'm not that hungry.' She forked a mouthful of salad, alternated it with the succulent fish, then took another sip of champagne in the hope it would renew her appetite.

'I've managed to get tickets for *Les Misérables*,' Michel remarked, and she offered him a smile.

'That's great.' She'd seen two different productions and loved both. 'When?'

'Tomorrow night.'

There was also a popular movie she wanted to see, and she mentioned it. 'Perhaps we could ask Angelina to join us?' she posed, aware how much pleasure it would give her stepsister. In which case she'd have to even things out by issuing a similar invitation to her stepbrother.

'Of course. But first, ascertain which night suits your mother and your father for dinner. As our guests.'

Step-family politics, she mused, required delicate handling.

It was almost ten when they left the restaurant, and within minutes Michel hailed a taxi to take them home.

Sandrine felt pleasantly tired as they entered the apartment, and she slid off her shoes and hooked the sling-back straps over one finger.

'Coffee?'

'I'll make it,' Michel offered as he shrugged out of his jacket. 'I need to go on-line and check some data.'

'Okay.' She tried to stem a feeling of disappointment. A part of her wanted to curl up in his arms and enjoy a leisurely lovemaking. Maybe she wouldn't be asleep when he came to bed, or if she was, he'd wake her. 'I'll go to bed and read.'

Except she only managed one chapter before the book slipped from her fingers and hit the carpeted floor, and she didn't stir when Michel slid quietly in beside her two hours later.

CHAPTER EIGHT

SANDRINE took the cordless phone into the bedroom after breakfast and rang her mother, had the call diverted to a mobile number and interrupted Chantal at the manicurist.

'Dinner, darling? Love to. How long are you in town?'

'A week, at least.'

'The weekend is out. Thursday?'

'Thursday's fine,' she agreed.

'Cristal. Seven o'clock? We'll meet you there.'

Her father was in a business meeting, but Lucas took the call, his conversation equally as brief as that of her mother.

'Friday,' Sandrine wrote in her diary planner.

That left Angelina and Ivan, step-siblings and arch-rivals for her attention. They were both in school and couldn't be contacted until late afternoon.

There were a few close friends she wanted to communicate with and she spent the next hour glued to the phone.

Michel was seated at the desk in the lounge when she emerged. The laptop was open, and he was speaking rapid French into his cell phone.

Sandrine wandered into the kitchen, poured herself

some fresh orange juice, then sat down at the dining-room table and leafed through the daily newspaper.

'What do you want to do with the day?' Michel queried when he finished his call.

'Me as in *me*?' she posed with a faint smile. 'Or me as in *you and me*?'

'You and me,' he drawled, reaching across to catch hold of her chin.

'Too much togetherness might not be wise.'

'You have me at your mercy. Choose.'

She pretended to consider as she ticked off each option on her fingers. 'The beach, a movie, shopping, wander around Darling Harbour, the Rocks, visit the Chinese Gardens, visit a few art galleries, the museum. Hmm,' she deliberated, then added without changing her voice, 'Or I could tie you to the bed and have my wicked way with you.' She sent him a stunning smile. 'Darling Harbour, I think. I'll go get changed.'

He tilted her chin and settled his mouth on hers in an all-too-brief evocative kiss. 'I'll take a raincheck.'

'On Darling Harbour?'

His eyes gleamed with latent humour. 'The bed.'

She slipped from his grasp. 'You did say I get to choose.'

It was a lovely day, with just enough of a breeze to take the edge off the summer's heat. Together they strolled along the boardwalk stretching the length of the Darling Harbour complex, enjoyed an excellent lunch at a waterfront restaurant, then browsed through the shops and crossed the pedestrian bridge. On impulse they took in a two-hour harbour cruise, then caught the monorail into the city.

It was almost six when they re-entered the apartment, and after a quick shower they each changed into elegant evening wear and took a taxi into the city.

There wasn't time for a leisurely meal, so they skipped the starter, settled for the main and forewent coffee in order to take their seats in time for the first act of *Les Misérables*.

It was a magnificent production, and Sandrine was lavish with her praise as they emerged into the foyer after the final act.

They chose a trendy café in which to have coffee, then hailed a taxi to the apartment.

Michel curved an arm round her waist as they stepped into the lift, and Sandrine rested her head against his shoulder. It had been a pleasant day, followed by a lovely evening, and she told him so.

'Thank you,' she added simply as they entered the lounge.

'For what, *chérie*? Spending a day with my wife?'

'For taking the time.'

He pulled her into his arms and kissed her, gently at first, then with increasing passion as she lifted her arms and wrapped them round his neck.

It was a while before he released her, and she stood there, his arms linked loosely around her hips, 'You're not going to check the laptop for messages?'

'There's nothing that can't wait until morning.'

She crossed to the wide hallway and made her way to the main bedroom, where she removed her shoes, the slim-fitting black gown and the beautifully crafted sequined jacket, then she reached to take the pins from her hair and encountered Michel's hand in the process of undoing the elegant French pleat.

When he was done, she helped him remove his jacket, the dress shirt, then the trousers. His eyes held hers as he slipped out of his shoes and peeled off his socks.

All that remained between him and total nudity was a pair of black hipster briefs, and she let her hand slide over his chest, teasing one male nipple, then the other, before skimming her fingers down to his waist.

She didn't tie him to the bed, but she did tease and tantalise him in a wicked exploration that tested the limit of his control. With her lips, the soft feather-light stroke of her fingers, the brush of her skin against his.

Sandrine lost track of time as she played the role of seductress, and just as he reached for her, she sank onto him and took his length in one exultant movement that shattered both of them.

What followed became a sweet, savage lovemaking that broke through the barriers of ecstasy and took them to a place where sensation ruled the mind, body and soul.

They went to sleep in each other's arms, and the last thing Sandrine remembered was the touch of Michel's lips against her temple, the deep, heavy tempo of his heart as it beat strongly in his chest.

Dinner with her mother, stepfather and Angelina carried undertones she was loath to pin down. Chantal was so incredibly vivacious it hurt, Roberto overdid the charm, and Angelina barely touched her food. Consequently the evening became something of a strain.

A call to her mother the next day brought an assurance Sandrine didn't buy for a second. It would do no good to question her father, and she didn't even bring up Chantal's name during dinner the following evening.

A shopping expedition on Saturday with Angelina brought forth a confidence that settled the question.

'Mum and Dad are getting a divorce,' Angelina blurted out as they shared lunch.

Sandrine experienced a gamut of emotions but managed to school most of them as she took in her stepsister's pinched features and lacklustre expression. 'How do you feel about it?' she queried gently.

'I hate it.'

I'm not that rapt, either, she echoed silently. Roberto may not be the ideal husband, but he was a caring father.

'She's seeing someone else,' Angelina informed her morosely.

'*She's* the cat's mother,' Sandrine corrected absently.

'*Mother*,' her stepsister declared with mocking emphasis, 'has a toy boy. I doubt he's thirty.'

Hell, that put a slightly different complexion on things. 'Maybe she's just—'

'Using him for sex?'

'Taking time out,' she continued, and wondered why she was trying to play down Chantal's behaviour to a sixteen-year-old who was more au fait with the situation.

'He drives a Ferrari, has oodles of money and looks like he stepped out of *GQ* wearing a Versace suit.'

Some contrast, when Roberto was on the wrong side of fifty, three stone overweight and losing his hair.

'And you hate him,' she deduced, and saw the younger girl work herself into a hissy fit.

'I hate *her*. What does she think she's *doing*? Dad practically lives at work, and I may as well not have sat my exams, the marks were so bad.'

Sandrine finished her *latte*. 'How long has this been going on?'

'Six months.'

'Okay.' She rose to her feet. 'Let's go.'

'Let's go? *That's it*?'

'Shopping.' She cast Angelina a purposeful smile. 'When the going gets tough, women go shopping.' She made a beckoning gesture. 'On your feet, girl. I'm about to indulge your wildest fantasy.'

Her stepsister's face was a study in conflicting emotions. 'You are?'

'Indeed.'

Sandrine was as good as her word, and when she had the taxi drop Angelina home early that evening, her stepsister was weighed down with a wide assortment of emblazoned carry bags.

'Thanks, Sandrine.' Angelina planted a kiss on her cheek before sliding out from the taxi. 'You're the best.'

No, Sandrine silently denied as the taxi swung back

into the flow of traffic. I merely trod the same path when Chantal and *my* father broke up, and I'd have given anything to have someone understand my pain.

She'd rung Michel from her cell phone to say she'd be late, and it was almost seven when she entered the apartment.

Michel met her at the door, saw her apparent tenseness and immediately cancelled plans he'd made for the evening. Instead, he brushed his lips across her forehead, then pushed her lightly in the direction of their bedroom.

'Go change, and I'll order in.'

Sandrine shot him a grateful glance. 'Pizza?'

'Okay.'

She kept walking, and in the bedroom she went into the en suite, took a leisurely shower, then she slipped on a short silk robe and pinned up her hair.

Michel sat sprawled on one of several sofas in the lounge, and he patted the seat beside him as she crossed the room. 'Come here.'

It would be heaven to receive some comfort, and she slid down onto the seat and curled her feet beneath her as he pulled her into the curve of his body.

'Want to tell me what's bothering you?'

Was she that transparent? Or was it because this man was so attuned to her that very little escaped him?

She told him briefly, wondering how anyone who hadn't shared a similar experience could possibly understand the breakdown of the family unit.

'You're concerned for Angelina.'

'The emotional upheaval has a far-reaching effect,'

Sandrine said slowly. 'It made me very aware of my own survival. I became very independent and self-contained. I guess I built up a protective shell.'

Yes, Michel agreed silently. She had at that, removing it for him, only to raise the barrier again at the first sign of discord. Self-survival... He was no stranger to it himself.

The intercom buzzed, and Michel answered it, releasing security for the pizza-delivery guy, and afterwards they bit into succulent segments covered with anchovies, olives, capsicum, mushrooms and cheese, washing them down with an excellent red wine while watching a romantic comedy on video.

The days that followed held a similar pattern. Michel divided the first half of each day to business via his laptop and cell phone, while Sandrine caught up with friends over coffee. Most evenings they dined out, took in a show or visited the cinema.

Sandrine's stepbrother, Ivan, chose the premiere screening of the latest *Star Wars* episode, and they indulged his preference for burgers and Coke.

Pinning down Chantal for a mother-and-daughter chat proved the most difficult to organise, with two lunch postponements. Third time lucky, Sandrine hoped as she ordered another mineral water from the waitress and half expected a call on her cell phone announcing Chantal's delay.

Fifteen minutes later Chantal slid into the chair opposite with a murmured apology about the difficulty of city parking and an express order for champagne.

'Celebrating, Chantal?' She hadn't called Chantal *Mother* since her early teens.

'You could say that, darling.'

'A new life?'

'Angelina told you,' Chantal said without concern, and Sandrine inclined her head.

'The news disturbed me.'

'It's my life to lead as I choose.'

'With a man several years younger than yourself?'

Chantal gave the waitress her order, then she leant back in her chair and took a long sip of champagne. 'I thought I was meeting my elder daughter for a chat over lunch.'

'I think I deserve some answers.'

'Why? It doesn't affect you in any way.'

That stung. 'It affects Angelina.' Just as your break-up with Lucas affected me.

'She'll get over it,' Chantal said carelessly. 'You did.'

Yes, but at what cost? It had succeeded in instilling such a degree of self-sufficiency that she thought only of herself, her needs and wants. And such a level of self-containment had almost cost her her marriage.

A slight shiver shook her slim frame. She didn't want to be like Chantal, moving from one man to another when she was no longer able to live life on her own terms. That wasn't love. It was self-absorption at its most dangerous level.

'This new man is—how old? Thirty?'

'Thirty-two.'

'Which means when you're sixty, he'll only be forty-four.'

'Don't go down that path, Sandrine,' Chantal warned.

'Why? Because you refuse to think that far ahead?'

'Because I only care about *now*.'

I don't, she noted with silent certainty. I care enough about the future to want to take care of every day that leads towards it. And I care about Michel enough to *want* a future with him. Desperately.

It was as if everything fell into place. And because it did, she chose not to pursue Chantal's indiscretions. Instead, she asked a string of the meaningless questions Chantal excelled in answering as they ate a starter and a main, then lingered over coffee.

They left the restaurant at three, promising to be in touch *soon*, and Sandrine took a page out of her own advice to Angelina. She went shopping. Nothing extravagant. A silk tie for Michel, despite the fact he owned sufficient in number to be able to wear a different one each day for several months. But she liked it and paid for it with a credit card linked to her own account and not the prestigious platinum card Michel had given her following their wedding.

'For you,' she said, presenting it to him within minutes of entering the apartment.

'*Merci, chérie.*'

'It's nothing much.'

His smile held a warmth that sent the blood coursing through her veins. 'The thought, *mignonne*, has more value than the gift itself.'

He pulled her into his arms and kissed her with such slow eroticism she almost groaned out loud when he released her.

'A call came through this afternoon. Tony wants you back on the set to reshoot a scene.'

Damn. Having to reshoot was something she'd been hoping to avoid. 'When?'

'Tomorrow. I've booked an early flight and accommodation at the Sanctuary Cove Hyatt.'

For the next few days the pace would be frenetic, she perceived. After the film wrapped, the publicity promotion would follow.

'Go change,' Michel bade her. 'We'll eat out, then get an early night.'

They chose an intimate French restaurant that served exquisite nouvelle cuisine, then afterwards they strolled along the street, pausing now and then to admire a shop window display. Michel threaded his fingers through her own, and with daylight-saving providing a late-evening dusk, the magic of pavement cafés and ornamental street lighting provided an illusory ambience.

Darkness fell, breaking the spell, and Michel hailed a cruising taxi to take them home.

CHAPTER NINE

IT HAD been a fraught day, Sandrine reflected as she garaged the car. Her final scene had to be shot again and again, and instead of being able to leave the set around midday, it was now almost seven.

She was tired, she had a headache, she was past hungry, and all she wanted to do was sink into a hot spa bath, slip on headphones and let the pulsing jets and music soothe her soul. For an hour.

Heaven, she breathed, entering the villa.

'I was just about to embark on a rescue mission,' Michel drawled as he strolled towards her. He took in her pale features, darkened eyes, the slight droop of her shoulders, and withheld an imprecation. 'Bad day?' he queried lightly. His hands curved over her shoulders as he drew her close. His mouth touched hers, lightly, briefly, and emotion stirred as she turned her face into the curve of his neck.

'Tony insisted the scene be shot so many times. I lost count after fifteen.' He smelt so good, *felt* so good, she could have stayed resting against him for ages. After a few timeless minutes she lifted her head and moved out of his arms. 'I'm going to soak in the tub.'

Warm water, scented oil, an Andrea Bocelli CD on the Walkman. Sandrine closed her eyes and let the tension gradually seep out of her bones.

She didn't hear Michel enter the bathroom, nor did she see him step into the tub, and the first indication she had was the light brush of fingers down her cheek.

Her eyelids flew wide and her mouth parted in unvoiced surprise as Michel positioned her in front of him.

She lifted a hand to remove the headphones only to have his hand close over hers holding them in place, then both hands settled on her shoulders and his fingers bit deep in a skilful massage that went a long way to easing the knots and kinks out of tense muscles.

She sighed blissfully as Michel handed her a flute of champagne, and she took a generous sip of the light golden liquid.

A slow warmth crept through her body, and with each subsequent sip she began to relax. Even her head felt light. Probably, she decided hazily, because she hadn't eaten a thing since lunch.

Sandrine had no idea how long she stayed in the gently pulsating water. It seemed ages, and she uttered a mild protest when the jets were turned off.

Michel lifted her from the tub, then caught up a large fluffy towel and dried the excess moisture from her body.

'You didn't have any champagne,' she murmured as he swept her into his arms and carried her into the bedroom.

'How do you feel?'

'Relaxed.'

He switched on the bedside lamp, hauled back the

bed covers and deposited her onto the sheeted mattress, then joined her.

All she wanted to do was curl into his arms, rest her head against his chest and absorb the strength and comfort he could offer her.

She felt his lips brush her own and she whispered his name in a semiprotest.

'Just close your eyes,' he bade huskily, 'and I'll do all the work.' His mouth grazed the edge of her jaw, then slipped down the slope of her throat.

What followed was a supplication of the senses as he embraced her scented skin with a touch as light as a butterfly's wing. With his lips, the pads of his fingers, he trailed a path from one sensory pleasure spot to another, lingering, savouring, until the warmth invading her body changed to slow-burning heat.

He lifted her hand and kissed each finger in turn, stroking the tip with his tongue, then when he was done he buried his mouth in her palm.

It was an evocative gesture that brought her response, only to have her touch denied as he completed a sensual feast that drove her wild.

He entered her slowly, and she groaned out loud as he initiated a long, sweet loving that was exquisite, magical. It left her weak-limbed and filled with languorous warmth.

Afterwards he folded her close into the curve of his body and held her as she slept. Her hair, loosened from its confining pins, spilled a river of silk over his pillow.

Michel waited a while, then carefully eased out of

bed, showered, dressed in jeans and a cotton shirt, then went downstairs to the kitchen and began organising the evening meal. He'd give her an hour, then wake her.

When he returned to the bedroom, she lay precisely as he'd left her, and he stood quietly at the foot of the bed for several minutes watching as she slept.

She possessed a fierce spirit, an independence that was laudable. It had been those very qualities that had drawn him to her, as well as her inherent honesty. His wealth didn't awe her, any more than *he* did. It was a rare quality to be liked for the man he was and not the Lanier family fortune.

Was she aware just how much she meant to him? She was the very air that he breathed, the daytime sun, the midnight moon.

Yet love alone wasn't enough, and he wasn't sufficiently foolish to imagine a ring and a marriage certificate were a guarantee of lifelong happiness.

Sandrine stirred, opened her eyes, focused on the man standing at the foot of the bed and offered him a slow, sweet smile.

'You shouldn't have let me sleep,' she protested huskily. 'What time is it?'

'Almost ten. Hungry?'

She didn't have to think about it. 'Ravenous.'

'I've made dinner.'

Surprise widened her eyes. 'You have?' She pushed herself into a sitting position and drew the sheet over her chest, then grinned at his teasing smile. 'Give me five minutes.'

She made it in seven, after the quickest shower on record, and slipped on a silky robe rather than dress.

'Oh, my,' Sandrine mused with pleasure as she sat down at the table. 'You do have hidden talent.'

'Singular?' Michel queried mockingly.

'Plural. Definitely plural,' she applauded as she sampled a sip of wine with a sigh of appreciation.

Filet mignon, delectable salad greens, a crusty baguette, and an excellent red wine, with a selection of fresh fruit.

Sandrine ate with pleasurable enjoyment, finishing every morsel on her plate, and she watched Michel cross to the stereo and insert a CD. Then he moved towards her and drew her up from the chair.

'What are you doing?' she queried with a faint laugh as he led her to the centre of the room and pulled her close.

The music was slow, the lyrics poignant, vocalized in the husky tones of a popular male singer.

Mmm, this was good, so good, she silently breathed as he cradled her body against his own. His hands stroked a sensuous pattern down her spine, then he cupped her bottom as she lifted her arms and linked her hands together at his nape.

The warmth of his body seemed to penetrate her own, and she melted into him as they drifted as one to the seductive tempo.

His lips settled at her temple, then slid down to the edge of her mouth, and she angled her head, inviting his possession in a kiss that was slow and so incredibly sweet she never wanted it to cease.

Sandrine gave a soundless gasp as he swept an arm beneath her knees and lifted her into his arms, then held on tight as he carried her through to the bedroom.

'Move, darling. Just a little closer now. Smile.'

If the photographer said *smile* one more time, she'd scream!

It was the end of what had been a very long day. Newspaper interviews and photographs from nine until eleven this morning, followed by a fashion shoot for the Australian edition of a top fashion magazine. Then an appearance at a high-profile charity luncheon held at the Sheraton Mirage, with a brief turn on the cat-walk.

There had been photographs at *Movieworld*. One of the prime television channels was videotaping coverage for a spot on the evening news.

Tonight was the gala black-tie event to publicise the movie. Dignitaries would be present, and the city's wealthy socialites would have paid handsomely to mix and mingle with the producer, director and actors.

It was all a planned marketing strategy to provide maximum impact in the publicity stakes. Gregor and Cait had given interviews in their hotel, and advertising trailers would run on television and in the cinemas.

Sandrine didn't have star status in the film, but as a home-grown talent in acting and modelling, she gained attention. As Michel Lanier's wife, she was guaranteed media coverage.

'Pretend, darling,' Cait murmured with a mocking edge. 'You're supposed to be an actress, so act.'

'As you do, *darling*?' she responded sweetly.

'She really is a barrel of laughs,' Gregor muttered to Sandrine sotto voce. 'Desperate, dateless and deadly.'

'I can have any man I want,' Cait ventured disdainfully.

'No,' he denied smoothly. 'Most, darling. But not all.'

'Go get stuffed.'

'I don't participate in anatomically impossible feats.'

'You could always try.'

'We'll move it over there,' the photographer called, indicating the marina and one luxury cruiser in particular, whose owner had generously lent it for publicity purposes.

How much longer before she could escape? Surely they didn't require her much longer?

'Okay, Sandrine, you can go. Cait, Gregor, I want a few inside shots.'

Thank heavens. She'd almost kill for a long, icy cold drink with just a dash of alcohol to soothe the day's rough edges.

'Lucky you,' Cait voiced cynically. 'You're off the hook.'

For now. She stepped off the cruiser and quickly cleared the marina. The adjoining luxury condominiums of the Palazzo Versace were spectacular in design, resembling a precious jewel set in a sparkling sapphire-blue sea.

Their hotel was reached via an overhead footbridge

from the shopping complex, and Sandrine went directly to their suite.

Michel was seated at the small desk, his shirt sleeves turned back, studying the screen on his laptop as she entered. He glanced at her, then raised an eyebrow as she moved straight to the bar fridge, extracted a bottle of sparkling fruit spritzer and rummaged through the assortment of miniature bottles in the minibar.

'That bad?' he queried as he rose to his feet and crossed to her side.

'Oh, yes.' She broke the seal on the gin, added a splash, then filled the glass with spritzer and took a long sip. 'And tonight will be worse.' She felt his hands on her shoulders and sighed as he skilfully worked the tense muscles there. 'Remind me we're flying out of here tomorrow.'

She heard his husky chuckle and leaned back against him. He felt so good she just wanted to close her eyes, absorb his strength and have the immediate world go away.

'Two days in Sydney,' he drawled, and brushed his lips to her temple. 'Then we fly home.'

Home had a nice ring to it. She pictured their New York apartment overlooking Central Park and sighed again, feeling some of the tension subside.

'I have a few things to tie up there, which will take a week, maybe longer, then we'll spend some time in Paris.'

'I think I love you,' Sandrine said fervently.

'Only *think, chérie*?'

She opened her mouth to protest, then closed it again. 'I was being facetious.'

'So one would hope.'

She turned slowly to face him, saw the gleam of humour evident in those dark eyes and aimed a loosely clenched fist at his chest. The next instant she cried out as he removed the glass from her fingers and hoisted her over one shoulder.

'What are you *doing*?'

He walked towards the adjoining en suite, released her down onto the tiled floor, then began removing her clothes, followed by his own.

'Michel?'

'Taking a shower.'

She glimpsed the slumberous passion evident and shook her head. 'We don't have time for this.'

He reached into the glassed shower cubicle and turned on the water, adjusted the temperature dial, then stepped inside and drew her with him. 'Yes, we do.'

The water beat down on her head, and she heard his husky chuckle as she cursed him. Then she stilled as he caught up the soap and ran it over her slim curves.

He was very thorough. Too thorough, Sandrine decided as heat flared through her body at his intimate touch, and she moaned out loud as his mouth closed over hers in an erotic tasting that almost sent her over the edge.

When he raised his head, she looked at him in dazed disbelief as he handed her the soap and encouraged her to return the favour.

She did, with such sensuous, lingering skill he lifted her high against him and plunged deep inside, again and again while she clung to him.

Afterwards he caught up the plastic bottle of shampoo and washed her hair, then rinsed it before shutting the water and reaching for both towels.

Dry, he pulled her close and kissed her with unabated passion, then put her firmly at arm's length.

Sandrine looked at him with musing suspicion. 'You planned that.' It was a statement, not a query.

'Guilty.'

She pulled the hair dryer from its wall attachment and switched it on. 'We'll be late.'

'No, we won't.'

Five minutes didn't count, Sandrine acknowledged less than an hour later as they entered the large downstairs foyer.

Michel looked striking in full evening dress, and she felt confident in encrusted ivory silk organza with a scooped neckline. Elegant evening pumps in matching ivory completed the outfit, and she'd swept her hair high in a smooth French pleat.

The function-room doors were open and guests were beginning to enter. The Gold Coast's social glitterati were evident in force, Sandrine perceived, noting the elegant gowns, expensive jewellery, exquisitely made-up and coiffed women present. Without exception, the men were in full evening dress and bow tie.

Sandrine sighted Stephanie, who returned her smile and joined them within seconds.

'I've seated you with Cait London, Gregor Anders,

the charity's chairwoman and her husband, and myself. The mayor and his wife are at Tony's table immediately adjoining yours. There'll be two tables seating the studio heads and various representatives from the marketing team.'

Sandrine saw Stephanie stiffen slightly and soon determined the reason as Raoul joined them.

'The photographer was happy with everything today,' Stephanie continued, ignoring Raoul after offering him a fleeting polite smile. 'There will, of course, be more taken tonight. However, we'll try to contain it so it doesn't become too intrusive. Now, if you'll excuse me?'

'You appear to have a disturbing effect on that young woman,' Michel observed to his brother.

'I'll settle for disturb rather than disinterest,' Raoul drawled in response, and Sandrine wrinkled her nose at her husband, then turned to Raoul.

'Like that, is it?' she teased.

'She doesn't want to talk to me and she avoids my calls.'

'I imagine you've arranged a few meetings with marketing?' she posed musingly, and glimpsed the gleam of humour evident in his expression. 'In Michel's absence, in the name of business, of course.'

His smile held a certain wry amusement. 'Of course.'

'Another rare young woman uninfluenced by the Lanier wealth and social status?'

'I think we should go inside and take our seats,'

Michel indicated quizzically. 'Naturally you've arranged to sit at our table?'

'*Oui*,' Raoul agreed dryly, and Sandrine suppressed a chuckle as a committee member checked their tickets and indicated their table location.

The chairwoman's husband was the sole occupant, and upon introduction he explained that his wife was busy with last-minute details. Of Cait and Gregor there was no sign, and Sandrine suppressed the uncharitable thought that Cait was probably aiming to stage-manage a dramatic entrance.

She wasn't wrong. Just as the lights flickered, indicating the formalities were about to begin, Cait swept into the function room with Gregor and a photographer in tow.

In a gown that was backless, strapless and appeared moulded to her figure, the actress stepped towards them, pausing every now and then to pose as the camera lens focused on her.

'We're not late, are we?' The beautiful, sultry smile was at variance with the breathless little-girl voice.

Cait, the actress, playing to the audience, Sandrine perceived wryly. Of the remaining empty seats, Cait slid into the one between Raoul and Michel.

Sandrine kept a smile in place with difficulty and took a sip of chilled wine.

Stephanie slipped into her seat seconds before the evening's master of ceremonies stepped on stage to take the microphone.

There were introductions and speeches as the spotlight focused on Cait, Gregor and Tony, followed by a studio representative. The mayor said his piece, then a small army of waiters began serving the starter as music beat through sound speakers and a singer provided entertainment on stage.

Sandrine was supremely conscious of the man seated at her side. His enviable aura of power combined with a dramatic measure of primitive sensuality had a magnetic effect.

Cait resembled a feline who'd just swallowed a saucer of cream, Sandrine observed as she forked a morsel of the artistically arranged starter.

'Darling, you don't mind if I have a few photos taken with Michel, do you?' Cait queried, managing to make the request sound like a statement.

The female star and the man who'd rescued a movie from financial disaster, Sandrine reflected cynically, and wondered why she should feel like a possessive tigress. Protecting your interest, a tiny voice taunted. And her interest was Michel, her marriage.

'Mr Lanier has specified any photographs in which he appears must also include his wife,' Stephanie informed her with businesslike candour.

'A group photo, perhaps?' Raoul suggested in a slightly accented drawl. 'Including the marketing manager?'

Stephanie cast him a level glance. 'I don't think that's necessary.'

'Oh, but I think it is,' Raoul argued smoothly. 'Marketing is an integral part of any film production, *non*?'

Careful, Sandrine cautioned silently. Stephanie is a

steel magnolia, not a fragile violet. Baiting her won't achieve a thing.

'Marketing as a whole,' Stephanie agreed.

The chemistry between them sizzled, Sandrine mused. Raoul was a persistent and determined man. While Stephanie gave every indication of wanting to avoid him at any cost. Who would win?

Michel reached out a hand and threaded his fingers through her own. She turned towards him and caught the smouldering passion evident beneath his veiled gaze.

'My money's on Raoul,' she said quietly.

'Indeed,' Michel agreed. 'Although I doubt it'll be an easy victory.'

His thumb began a disturbing pattern across the sensitive veins inside her wrist, an action that played havoc with her equilibrium. As he intended it to do.

'I think I need to repair my make-up,' Sandrine ventured, and caught Michel's knowing smile. He realized the effect he had on her and precisely why she wanted a temporary escape.

'You look beautiful just the way you are.'

'Flattery won't get you anywhere,' she responded with a teasing smile, aware that she lied. She was so incredibly susceptible to everything about him. His voice, the softly spoken French he frequently lapsed into whenever he became lost in the throes of passion. The fluid movement of his body, his limbs, the way he smiled and those chiselled features softened when he looked at her.

She'd thought independence was important, but

nothing in her life held a candle to her love for Michel. He'd been right from the start. Why choose to be apart unless circumstances made it impossible to be together?

All those lonely nights she'd spent in her empty bed she'd longed for him to be beside her, to feel his touch. She'd enjoyed the part she'd played in the film, but that satisfaction didn't come close in compensation for being away from her husband.

Sandrine pushed open the door to the powder room and freshened up. Just as she was about to leave, Cait entered the vestibule.

One eyebrow slanted in recognition, and her mouth curved into a petulant smile. 'Really, darling, I'm surprised you could bear to leave Michel's side.'

Sandrine was heartily sick of the actress's game playing. 'It's a challenge, is it, Cait, to seduce another woman's husband?'

'Forbidden fruit, darling, tastes much sweeter than any that's readily available.' She raised a hand and placed the tip of a finger in her mouth. 'And it's always interesting to see if I can pluck the fruit from the tree.' She deliberately licked her finger, removed it, then offered Sandrine a sultry look. 'So to speak.'

Sandrine had had enough. She replaced her powder sponge and lipstick in her bag and closed the clasp. 'If you can succeed with Michel, you can have him.' She moved towards the door and paused momentarily at the sound of Cait's sultry drawl.

'Aren't you going to wish me good luck?'

'The hell I will,' she said inelegantly, and stepped quickly to the function room.

The buzz of voices hit her the moment she re-entered the large room, and she forced herself to walk slowly across the carpeted floor.

The chairwoman and her husband were absent from their table, as were Stephanie and Gregor. Only Michel and Raoul remained, and they appeared deep in conversation as she rejoined them.

Michel cast her a quick glance, glimpsed the faint edge of tension and accurately defined the reason for it.

'Cait?'

She managed a wry smile. 'She made it clear you're the target of her affections.'

'Indeed.'

He seemed amused, damn him.

'If you choose to play her game, then she can have you.'

He picked up her hand and lifted it to his lips, then kissed each finger in turn. 'Now why would I do that, *chérie*, hmm?' He grazed his teeth against her thumb, and saw her eyes flare. 'When all I want is you.'

'Perhaps you should tell Cait that.'

He brushed his mouth across the delicate veins inside her wrist, and Sandrine barely controlled the shiver that threatened to scud the length of her spine.

She could feel herself slowly drowning when she looked at him. The liquid warmth evident in his gaze rendered her bones to jelly, and she had to physically stop herself from leaning forward to place her lips against the sensuous curve of his mouth.

As crazy as it seemed, she could almost feel him inside her, relive the strength and the power of him as muscles deep inside clenched and unclenched in intimate spasms.

He knew. She could see by the glint of those dark eyes that he'd somehow detected the way she was inwardly reacting to him. She lowered her lashes and attempted to pull her hand free. To no avail, as he merely carried her hand to rest on his thigh.

An equally dangerous move, and she pressed the tips of her fingernails into hard muscle in silent warning.

'We've been invited to party on at the hotel's nightclub,' Michel relayed. 'Everyone else associated with the film and marketing will be there.'

She almost groaned out loud. 'Tell me our flight isn't the early-morning one,' she pleaded, and he gave a husky laugh.

'Eleven-thirty.'

'Breakfast before nine isn't an option,' she warned.

'Plan on sleeping in, *chérie*?'

She wrinkled her nose at him. '*Sleep* is the operative word.'

The photographer got his shots, several of them. Raoul very cleverly positioned himself beside Stephanie while Cait insinuated herself between Raoul and Michel. Gregor, bless him, wriggled his eyebrows at them all and flanked Stephanie.

It was after eleven when the evening began to wind

down, and half an hour later they wandered in groups towards the nightclub.

The DJ was spinning loud, funky music, the air was thick with noise, a cacophony of voices straining to be heard, and flashing strobe lighting provided a visual disturbance.

'Let's party, darling,' Gregor invited as he swept a glass of wine from the tray of a passing waitress.

'Why don't you ask Sandrine to dance?' Cait queried with a contrived pout. 'I want to play with the big boys.'

'Both of whom have their own women,' Gregor warned, regardless of her careless shrug. 'Don't do it, sweetheart.'

'Oh, stop trying to spoil my fun.'

Raoul turned towards Stephanie and indicated the crowded dance floor. 'Are you game to enter the fray?'

'With you?'

'Of course with me.'

'I'm not really into dancing.'

Cait placed a hand on Michel's forearm and used her fingers to apply a little pressure as she tilted her head and offered a provocative smile. 'Sandrine won't mind if I drag you away.' She turned towards Sandrine, openly daring her to object. 'Will you, darling?'

Michel covered Cait's hand with his own and transferred it to her side. His expression was polite, but there was an inflexible hardness apparent in his gaze. 'Regrettably, I do mind.'

Cait didn't bat an eyelash. 'I think the idea is for

everyone to loosen up a little now the film is in the can.'

'Define "loosen up",' Michel drawled.

Sandrine recognised the faint inflection in his voice and almost felt sorry for Cait.

'There's the party after the party, if you know what I mean,' the actress intimated with deliberate coquetry. 'A very *private* party.'

Was she aware just how brazen she sounded? And how damning? There was an edge apparent, a hyped overbrightness that hinted at substance enhancement. It left a sick feeling in Sandrine's stomach and provoked a degree of sadness.

'No.'

Cait's mouth formed a perfect bow. 'No?'

If she stayed another minute, she'd say something regrettable! 'Please, excuse me for a few minutes?'

'Do you mind if I join you?' Stephanie asked.

It took several minutes to weave their way through the nightclub patrons and locate the powder room. Once inside, the noise level diminished to a bearable level as they joined the queue waiting to use the facilities.

'Ten minutes, fifteen tops,' Stephanie commented as she examined her nails. 'Then I'm out of here, business and social obligations completed.'

'The suits won't have reason to complain,' Sandrine agreed with a quizzical smile, then saw the marketing manager visibly relax.

'It's all coming together well. The trailers are good, and the media blitz will gain the public's attention.'

The queue shifted, and they moved forward a few paces.

'I understand you're returning to Sydney tomorrow.'

Sandrine inclined her head. 'Just for a few days, then we fly home.'

'New York,' Stephanie murmured. 'I visited there once. Very fast, very cosmopolitan.'

'It has a beat all its own.'

'Distinctive.'

'Like the Lanier men.'

'One of them in particular,' Stephanie declared dryly.

Sandrine shot her a teasing smile. 'Persistent, is he?' she queried, and caught the other woman's wry grimace.

'You could say that.'

'Naturally, you don't like him.'

'He makes me feel uncomfortable.'

'Uncomfortable is good.'

'No,' Stephanie refuted. 'It's a pain in the neck.'

A light bubble of laughter rose to the surface. 'Good luck.'

'For Raoul to catch me? Or for me to escape unscathed?'

'Oh, I'll take a gamble and go for the first option,' Sandrine said wickedly.

'Not in this lifetime.'

There was a finality about those few words, and she wondered what, or rather *who* had damaged Stephanie's trust in men.

The music hit them in waves as they returned to the nightclub, and Stephanie joined a representative group from the marketing team as Sandrine crossed to rejoin Michel.

As she approached, Cait wound an arm round his neck and placed her mouth to his. It was a deliberate and calculated action, she knew, but one that angered her unbearably.

Michel showed restrained dignity as he broke the contact, and the actress turned towards Sandrine with a tantalising smile.

'You said I could have him, darling.'

'From where I stood, it didn't look as if he wanted you,' she managed in a remarkably even voice.

'Bitch.'

'I could say the same.'

Michel caught Sandrine's hand and linked his fingers through hers, applying a slight warning pressure. Which she ignored.

'Perhaps we should leave,' he suggested indolently, and suppressed a degree of amusement as Sandrine shot him a stunning smile.

'Why? I'm having so much fun.' She lifted his hand and brushed her lips across his knuckles. 'Ask me to dance.'

His eyes darkened and acquired a wicked gleam as he led her onto the dance floor. 'Minx,' he murmured close to her ear.

'Confrontation,' she mocked lightly. 'Works so much better than retreat.' A light gasp escaped her lips as he drew her in close. 'That might be a bit of overkill.' One hand cupped her bottom while the other slid to clasp her nape.

'You think so?' he drawled, enjoying the way her heart thudded into a quickened beat, the slight huskiness in her voice.

The music slowed, and they drifted together for several long minutes, only to break apart as the DJ switched discs and tempo.

By mutual consent they began circulating between the various business heads from marketing, the studio. Something that took a while, until they came at last to Raoul.

'Sleep well,' she bade as he brushed his lips to her cheek.

Minutes later they entered their suite, and Sandrine slipped off her shoes, then unfastened the zip and stepped out of her gown.

It had been a long day, and there was a sense of satisfaction that everything had come to a close.

She crossed to the en suite, removed her make-up, slipped on a silk nightshirt, then re-entered the bedroom and slid into bed.

Within seconds Michel joined her, snapped off the bedlamp, then caught her close.

It was heaven to lean against him, to feel the reassuring beat of his heart beneath her cheek. His lips touched her temple, then slid to her mouth to bestow a brief, warm kiss.

His chin rested against the top of her head, and she simply closed her eyes and drifted off to sleep within seconds.

CHAPTER TEN

SYDNEY looked achingly familiar, and the Double Bay apartment particularly welcoming. There were several things she wanted to do, a few loose ends she needed to tie up, and she wanted some time alone with her father.

Michel's cell phone rang as Sandrine began unpacking the few necessities required during the next day or two, and his voice faded into a muted sound as he took the call in the lounge.

He returned to the bedroom minutes later and began unpacking. 'Raoul has set up a meeting with the Enrique Corporation for tomorrow afternoon.'

A new deal, initiated by Raoul who had flown into Sydney the previous day, which, if it proved successful, would see a Lanier Corporation link in Australia.

'I'll ring Lucas and see if he's free to meet me for lunch.'

Michel handed her his cell phone. 'Do it now. We're meeting Raoul for dinner, and it might be late when we get back.'

She punched in the relevant numbers, greeted her father's availability with enthusiasm and agreed on a time and place to meet.

'All done,' Sandrine said with satisfaction. She had

twenty minutes in which to change and repair her make-up, and she managed it with a minute to spare.

Deep red evening trousers and a matching cropped evening jacket worn over a black silk camisole highlighted the texture of her skin and emphasised the lustrous colour of her hair. She left it loose to fall onto her shoulders, simply because there wasn't sufficient time to pin it up.

Raoul was booked into the Ritz-Carlton in Double Bay, and they joined him in the lounge at seven for a drink before entering the restaurant.

The maître d' led them to a table and snapped his fingers for the wine steward.

'Too premature for champagne?' Sandrine queried with a quizzical smile.

'Who needs a special occasion to drink champagne? Dom Pérignon,' Raoul instructed, and she observed the smooth approach of the waiter. Such synchronisation in service deserved a reward.

After they ordered a starter and main, deferring dessert, Sandrine spared a cursory glance at the room and its occupants as she sipped champagne from a crystal flute.

Michel and Raoul discussed strategy for the next day's meeting and finetuned arrangements over the starter.

They were part way through the main dish when something caught Sandrine's attention. The stark light of a flashbulb, followed by the glimpse of a familiar figure combined with a trill of laughter she'd hoped never to hear again.

For a moment she thought, *hoped* she was mistaken, but no, there, making a grand entrance, was none other than Cait London.

I don't believe this. She had known Cait and Gregor were due to fly out to the States this week, but of all the hotels in Sydney, was it coincidence Cait had chosen this one...or had she done some careful sleuthing?

Perhaps she wouldn't notice they were here?

Fat chance, Sandrine acknowledged in wry silence as she viewed Cait's performance. For it was a piece of superb acting, which didn't fool her in the slightest. Any more than it deceived Michel or Raoul as Cait approached their table.

'For heaven's sake,' Cait greeted with delighted enthusiasm, 'who would have thought we'd run into each other, *here*, of all places.'

The maître d' hovered, well used to the presence of celebrities in this exclusive hotel. He aimed to please and to serve, and Cait took flagrant advantage of his position.

'You don't mind if I join you?' She slid into the chair held out for her, then waved her hand in an elegant gesture to the wine steward. 'Bring another bottle of champagne.' When the waiter presented her with a menu, she scanned it quickly, then handed it back to him. 'Just a starter. The Caesar salad.'

'You're alone?' Raoul drawled in query, and Sandrine watched Cait weigh up which Lanier brother she'd attempt to captivate.

Just try it with Michel, she warned silently, and I'll scratch your eyes out!

The famous pout was a touch overdone. 'Gregor deserted me, the rat.' Her mouth formed a moue. 'I could have ordered room service, but I didn't feel like being alone.'

Cashing in on national publicity and revelling in the limelight, Sandrine perceived, then mentally chastised herself for being cynical.

'So, what are we celebrating?'

'Life,' Michel stated with studied indolence as he took hold of Sandrine's hand and lifted it to his lips. 'And love.' He kissed each fingertip in turn, then curled her hand within his.

Oh, my, that was about as blatant as you could get. Add to that the passionate gleam apparent in his eyes, the sensual curve of his lips. It was a combination that succeeded in melting her bones.

'Quite a change from when Michel first appeared on the scene a month ago,' Cait imputed with thinly veiled sarcasm. 'At Tony's apartment I could have sworn you were enemies instead of husband and wife.'

'If husbands and wives didn't experience a difference of opinion on occasion, the marriage would become boring,' Sandrine offered.

'Really?'

'Anyone for coffee?' Raoul intervened. 'I have a few calls to make.'

'Likewise I need to go on-line.' Michel succeeded in attracting the maître d's attention, then turned towards Cait. 'By all means stay on and finish the champagne.'

They weren't able to escape quite so easily. The

photographer appeared out of nowhere and reeled off a few shots, which, unless Sandrine was mistaken, would be sold to at least one of the national newspapers.

Michel muttered an imprecation beneath his breath, signed the proffered credit slip, then rose to his feet and pocketed his wallet.

'Safe flight, darlings,' Cait bade, again looking like a cat who'd just finished a bowl of cream.

'*Merci.*'

Michel curved an arm round Sandrine's waist as Raoul accompanied them to the main entrance, then waited as they slid into a taxi.

'Coincidence, do you think?' she posed as the taxi swiftly joined the traffic.

'Extremely doubtful,' Michel said dryly.

'Coffee?' Sandrine offered on entering the apartment five minutes later. 'We didn't have any, and if you need to work on-line...'

'The only thing I want to work closely with is *you.*'

A lazy grin widened her mouth, and her eyes sparkled as she turned towards him. 'I'm not sure I like being referred to as a *thing.*'

He crooked a finger in a beckoning gesture. 'Come here.'

Laughter bubbled up inside her, emerging as a delightful throaty sound. 'You'd better have a good reason for issuing orders.'

'Oh, I don't think you'll have reason to complain.'

She moved into his arms and felt them enfold her close. 'Really?'

'*Really*,' he mocked lightly, then proceeded to kiss her with such passion she went up in flames.

They made it to the bedroom, discarding clothes as they went, and it was a long time before she found the energy to do more than murmur her appreciation as she slipped close to the edge of sleep.

The taxi eased to a halt outside the Ritz-Carlton, and Michel paid the driver as Sandrine emerged from the vehicle.

Together they entered the main lobby, shared a coffee with Raoul, then Sandrine rose to her feet and brushed Michel's temple with a light kiss.

'Three o'clock?'

Michel's answering smile held warmth as he inclined his head. 'Have fun.'

Her mouth assumed a wicked curve. 'I intend to.' She wanted to select a special gift for his grandmother and she was due to meet her father at one.

Double Bay was a delightful place to browse and shop, and she found a beautiful Hermès silk scarf that was just perfect.

It was almost one when she entered the restaurant Lucas had recommended, and she was barely seated when the maître d' showed him to their table.

'Sandrine,' Lucas greeted with affection, 'this is a pleasure.'

She ordered wine, and they settled on a starter and main.

'It's regrettable this has to be brief, but I have a scheduled meeting at two-fifteen.'

'That's okay,' Sandrine voiced without hesitation.

He surveyed her over the rim of his glass. 'You have something on your mind you want to discuss with me?'

'Chantal.'

Lucas replaced his glass down on the table. 'You know your mother and I no longer maintain contact.'

She was aware of all the reasons why and had accepted them. 'I'm concerned for her.'

'And you expect me to share that concern?'

'She's my mother,' she said simply.

'Chantal is an emotional butterfly, always seeking something different and new. When life becomes boring, she moves on without too much thought for those left behind.' He paused as the waiter removed their plates. 'I rebuilt my life with a loving woman.'

A loving woman who was civil and superficially affectionate to her husband's daughter from his first marriage, but one who'd made it clear Sandrine had no place in her home or her heart.

Lucas placed a hand over hers. 'Your mother will never change. She's *Chantal*,' he declared with wry cynicism, as if that explained it all. 'You have Michel. Treasure that love and treat it with care.'

There was no point to pursuing the conversation, and she didn't even try. Instead, they spoke of Ivan's academic achievements and aspirations.

It was after two when they emerged from the restaurant, and Sandrine gave her father an affectionate hug in farewell.

She needed to make a few calls to friends, and she

strolled towards the hotel, settled herself comfortably in the lounge, ordered a cappuccino and punched a series of numbers into her cell phone.

She temporarily lost track of time, and it wasn't until she glanced at her watch after concluding the last of her calls that she realised it was after three.

Where was Michel? Sandrine checked her watch for the third time in fifteen minutes. It wasn't like him to be late.

'Can I get you anything else, ma'am?'

She cast the waitress a brief smile and shook her head. 'Thank you.'

A slight frown creased her forehead. She hadn't got the meeting place wrong because Michel had dropped her off outside this hotel more than three hours ago.

Perhaps he'd been held up. Yes, that was it. His meeting had run overtime.

The frown deepened. If that were true, why didn't he ring? She slipped the cell phone from her bag and checked it for any messages. There were none.

Okay, she'd ring him on his cell phone. A few words of reassurance were all she needed. Without further hesitation she punched in the numbers and waited, only to have the call switch to voice mail. She left a message, then slipped the phone into her bag.

Raoul. Maybe she could call Raoul, she thought, only to remember she hadn't keyed his number into her memory bank.

Business lunches were notorious for running late. Any minute now Michel would call, apologise and explain. Except he didn't, and a fist closed over her heart.

Several different scenarios played through her mind and she examined and discarded each of them.

The peal of the phone interrupted her increasing apprehension, and she plucked the unit from her bag and activated it.

'Raoul, Sandrine.'

'Michel—'

'Is okay,' Raoul assured her. 'There was a slight car accident, and the officers who attended the scene insisted everyone involved receive a medical examination.'

Dear heaven. 'Where?'

He named a private city hospital. 'Take a cab. I'll be waiting for you.'

A chill invaded her bones. 'I'm on my way.'

The ensuing fifteen minutes were the longest minutes of her life as she imagined a plethora of possibilities regarding Raoul's description of events.

'Okay, he's okay,' she repeated several times beneath her breath as the cab negotiated heavy city traffic.

What if Raoul wasn't telling her the truth? Dear Lord in heaven, what if the accident had been severe?

Sandrine froze. Images of horrific televised accident scenes flashed before her eyes. She pictured bodies being cut from crushed vehicles and transported by ambulance to hospital.

How much longer? She checked the location and estimated another five minutes should do it, providing there were no unexpected traffic snarls.

The cab made it in seven, and she hurriedly thrust

a note into the driver's hand, opened the door and
waved away his move to give her change.

She ran down the concrete path and paused impa-
tiently as she waited for the automatic glass doors of
the main entrance to open.

Sandrine was oblivious to the nurses' station, the
collection of waiting patients. All she saw was Raoul
crossing the room towards her, and she rushed to his
side.

'He's with the doctor,' Raoul soothed, taking hold
of her elbow as he led her down a corridor. 'He's fine.
The wound needs a few stitches.'

Her stomach clenched at the thought of torn flesh
being stitched together. 'How bad is it?'

Raoul gave her arm a reassuring squeeze. 'A few
scratches, some bruising.' He indicated a doorway to
the right. 'He's in here.'

Sandrine's heart missed a beat, then thudded loudly
in her chest as she stepped into the room. The attending doctor partly obscured Michel from her view, and
she moved quickly to his side, her eyes sweeping over
his features, his lengthy frame, in a bid to determine
the extent of his injuries.

'*Michel*,' she breathed raggedly as she took in those
flawless, broad-boned facial features, then roved over
his bare chest.

No scratches, no visible bruising, she noted with
relief. The doctor was working on Michel's left arm,
stitching what looked to be a deep gash, and she paled
at the sight of the needle suturing the wound.

'My wife,' Michel drawled as the doctor paused in his task to give her a quick glance.

'Your husband is fine. A few bruised ribs from the restraining seat belt, plus a gashed arm. I'll be done in a few minutes, then you can take him home.'

Sandrine felt the blood drain from her face as her vivid imagination envisaged the car screeching as Michel applied the brakes, the sickening crunch as two cars collided, the reflexive action at the moment of impact.

For one brief, infinitesimal second she experienced a mental flash of how it might have been, and the thought of what *could* have happened almost destroyed her. A life without Michel in it would be no life at all.

A hand curved round her nape as Michel pulled her towards him, and her hands instinctively clutched hold of his shoulders. Then his mouth was on hers in a brief, hard kiss that almost immediately softened to a light caress before he released her.

'Don't, *chérie*,' he chastised huskily, and uttered a muffled curse as he saw her lips tremble.

She tried to smile but didn't quite make it.

Michel's eyes darkened, and he caught her hand and held it. His thumb lightly caressed the veins inside her wrist, moving in a rhythmic pattern that stirred her senses. Just looking at him made her want to fling her arms around him and hold on tight.

Relief flooded her veins, closely followed by love. The deep, abiding-forever kind. Her heart, her emotions, belonged to this man, unequivocally. Nothing else held any importance.

'There, all done,' the doctor declared as he applied a dressing and secured it. 'Those stitches need to be removed in a week.'

Michel rose to his feet, grabbed his shirt from the back of the chair, shrugged it on and attended to the buttons before slipping into his jacket. 'Let's get out of here.'

'I'll organise the cab and drop you off on my way to the airport,' Raoul stated as they exited the building, and Sandrine gave him a brief, keen glance.

'You're flying back to the Gold Coast?'

He offered her a wry smile. 'Yes.'

'I see.'

'Do you?'

Her eyes held musing humour. 'Oh, yes.' Stephanie was in for a battle if she thought she could easily dismiss Raoul. The Lanier men fought for what they wanted. 'I recognise the signs.'

'Then wish me luck, Sandrine.'

'Do you need it?'

His expression assumed a faint bleakness.

So he wasn't so sure after all. Good, she decided silently. He'd appreciate Stephanie all the more for not providing him with an easy victory.

She lifted a hand and brushed her fingers down that firm cheek. 'You have it, Raoul.'

He offered her a smile that held warmth and affection. '*Merci.*'

CHAPTER ELEVEN

THERE was a rank of taxis outside the main entrance, and one moved forward at a flick from Michel's fingers.

Twenty minutes later the cab slid to a halt outside their apartment building, and they bade Raoul a quick farewell, then made their way through the foyer to the lift.

The instant the lift doors closed behind them, Michel punched the appropriate panel button, then he pulled her close and fastened his mouth over hers in a kiss that was all too brief as the doors slid open at their designated floor. They walked the few steps to their door and then entered the apartment.

For a few seconds she stood in dazed silence, her eyes large as she looked at him. There was so much she wanted to say, yet the words seemed caught in her throat.

He was so dear to her, so very special. Life itself. Without him, the flame within her would flicker and die.

Something flared in his eyes, and she stood perfectly still as he threaded his fingers into her hair and tilted her head.

'I couldn't bear to lose you,' she said simply, and saw his lips curve into a gentle smile.

'It isn't going to happen.'

'Today, just for a while, I thought it might have.'

As long as he lived, he'd never forget the expression in her eyes, the paleness of her features when she entered the emergency room. His thumb caressed the firm line of her jaw. 'I know.'

She swallowed, the expression in her eyes mirroring her emotions. 'You probably should rest,' she voiced huskily.

'You think so?'

'Michel...' She paused as his head lowered down to hers and his lips settled on one cheekbone, then began trailing a path down the slope of her jawbone to settle at the edge of her mouth.

'Hmm?'

'I can't think when you do that.'

'Is it so important that you think?'

One hand moved to the vee of her top and slid beneath it.

'I want...' Her breath hitched as his fingers brushed the slope of her breast, the touch infinitely erotic over the soft silk and lace of her bra.

His lips teased hers, light as a butterfly's wing, as they stroked over the sensuous lower curve, then he swept his tongue to taste the sweetness within.

This, *this*, was where she was meant to be. Held in the arms of the man who was her soul mate. Nothing else mattered.

'What is it you want, *chérie*?' Michel drawled gently.

'*You*,' she said simply. 'But first...' Her voice

climbed a few notches, then came to a sudden halt as his fingers slid to unfasten the clip of her bra. The sensitive peaks burgeoned in anticipation of his touch, and heat arrowed from deep within as he began an erotic, evocative stroking. It drove her wild, and she groaned out loud as he pulled the knit top over her head, discarded her bra, then lowered his mouth to one highly sensitised peak.

She could feel herself begin to melt as her body melded to his, aligning itself to allow him access as her hands crept round his neck.

A long, heartfelt sigh whispered from her lips as he shifted his attention to render a similar salutation to its twin. For what seemed an age she exulted in the sheer sensation his touch evoked, feeling every pore, every nerve cell pulse into vibrant life.

It wasn't enough, and she murmured encouragement when his fingers slipped to her waist and attended to the zip fastening.

His clothes were an impossible barrier she sought to remove with considerable care, and his gentle smile almost completely undid her as he put her at arm's length and finished the task.

Sandrine took in his muscled frame, the olive-toned skin stretching over superb bone structure and honed sinew. His shoulders were broad, his chest tightly muscled and liberally sprinkled with dark, curling hair that arrowed down to his waist, then flared into a geometric vee at the juncture of his thighs.

He was an impressive, well-endowed man, a skilled and exciting lover whose degree of *tendresse* melted her bones, while his passion had the power to awe and overwhelm.

With one easy movement he swept an arm beneath her knees and lifted her high against his chest.

'Your arm,' she protested, and heard his husky laughter.

'Afraid it might hinder me?' Michel teased as he strode through to the bedroom.

'Hurt you,' she corrected as he pulled back the bed-clothes and drew her down with him onto the sheets.

He kissed her, deeply and with such soul-destroying intensity she lost track of time and place until he slowly released his mouth from her own.

She looked *kissed*, he saw with satisfaction. Her mouth was slightly swollen, and her eyes resembled huge liquid pools a man could drown in.

He wanted to savour the taste of her, skim his lips over every inch of her skin, suckle at her breasts with the ferocity of a newborn infant seeking succour. Except a man nurtured his woman's breasts to give her pleasure, for some of the most sensitised nerve endings were centred at those peaks.

Most of all he wanted to bury himself deep in her moist heat and become lost in the sweet sorcery that was *Sandrine*. His woman, his wife. His life.

From the moment he met her, he had only one agenda. It was instant, breathtaking desire. Yet it had been more than that, much more. Deep within the raw, primitive emotion had been the instinctive knowledge they were meant to be. Almost as if they'd known each other in a former existence.

Crazy, he dismissed with a mental shake of his head. He possessed a logical, analytical mind. Yet he was frighteningly aware of the timing and how, had he not been at a friend's home attending a party, he might never have met her. Equally, the slender thread of chance that led her to be persuaded to tag along to something she freely admitted hadn't been her first choice of an evening's entertainment.

Of the many women he'd met socially and in the business arena, there had been none who'd come close to the magic that was Sandrine.

Beautiful, with a gently curving slenderness that made her frame perfect for displaying designer clothes on various European catwalks. Fine-boned facial features, lovely, wide-spaced dark brown eyes, a generous mouth.

Rather than her physical appearance, it had been the genuine warmth of her smile, the expressive eyes and her *joie de vivre*. The way her chin tilted when she laughed, the faint twist of her head as she tossed her hair back over her shoulders. The sound of her voice, its faint huskiness when she became emotionally aroused. And because he was a man, the feel of her body in his arms, her mouth beneath his. The scent and essence that made her unique.

Destined to be, he mused, like two halves of a whole that fitted perfectly together as one.

'Michel?'

He looked down at her and tried to control the slight tremor that threatened to destroy the slim hold on his libido. 'You get to talk *after* we make love,' he teased mercilessly, and felt his body go weak at the languorous humour evident in those beautiful dark eyes.

'You could make an exception.'

He trailed a finger down the slope of her nose. 'So what is it you want to say that can't wait, hmm?'

She reached up a hand and pressed a finger to his lips, stilling any words he might have added. '*I love you.*' There was the prick of unshed tears, an ache deep inside her heart.

He kissed each of her fingers in turn, and she almost melted from the warmth evident in his gaze. '*Merci, chérie,*' he said gently.

'I always have,' she assured him with such a depth of feeling two tears materialised, clung to her lashes, then spilled to run down her cheek in twin rivulets. 'I always will.'

His thumb stroked away the dampness. 'Are you done?'

She inclined her head and made an attempt to restore her composure. Her gaze speared his, and there was a depth apparent that made him catch his breath.

'I have something for you.' He reached out and slid open a drawer of the bedside pedestal, extracted something, then turned back to her and caught hold of her left hand.

It was an exquisite diamond-studded ring, a perfect complement to her existing rings.

'It's beautiful,' Sandrine breathed. 'Thank you.' A circle symbolising eternity. She wanted to cry. 'I have nothing for you.'

The passionate warmth evident in his gaze succeeded in melting her bones. 'You're wrong,' Michel said tenderly. '*You* are my gift. Infinitely more precious than anything you could give me. *Je t'aime, mon amour.*' His voice was husky as he curved her close against him. '*Je t'adore.*' His lips hovered fractionally above her own. 'You are my life, my love. Everything.'

Love was understanding, compassion and trust. And more, much more.

She linked her hands behind his head and pulled him down to her. '*Merci*,' she teased, and heard his husky growl an instant before his mouth closed over hers.

After the loving, she lay spent, curled in against his side, one arm flung across his midriff, her cheek resting on his chest.

The sun had shifted lower in the sky, and soon dusk would fall. Shadows danced slowly across the pale wall, creating an indecipherable pattern.

At last everything had fallen into place, she decided dreamily. The film was finished, publicity completed. Tomorrow she would board a flight with Michel bound for New York. A week later they'd embark on a holiday in France.

Paris in winter, drizzle, grey skies. But nothing would dull the magic of love in a city made for lovers. It was the appropriate city in which to try to conceive a child.

'Are you awake?'

She felt him shift slightly towards her. 'Want me to order in something to eat?'

'How do you feel about children?'

'In general?'

She waited a few seconds. 'Ours.'

Now she had his attention. 'Are you trying to tell me something?'

'There's nothing to tell...yet.'

He propped up his head as he leant towards her. 'The thought of your being pregnant with my child overwhelms me.'

She wrinkled her nose at him. 'Too overwhelming?'

He kissed her with lingering thoroughness. 'I think we should work on it.'

'Now?'

'You object?'

She didn't answer. Instead, she showed him just how she intended to work on it.

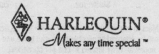

Back by popular demand are

DEBBIE MACOMBER's

Hard Luck, Alaska, is a
town that needs women!
And the O'Halloran brothers
are just the fellows
to fly them in.

Starting in March 2000 this beloved series returns
in special 2-in-1 collector's editions:

MAIL-ORDER MARRIAGES, featuring
Brides for Brothers and *The Marriage Risk*
On sale March 2000

FAMILY MEN, featuring
Daddy's Little Helper and *Because of the Baby*
On sale July 2000

THE LAST TWO BACHELORS, featuring
Falling for Him and *Ending in Marriage*
On sale August 2000

Collect and enjoy each MIDNIGHT SONS story!

Available at your favorite retail outlet.

HARLEQUIN®
Makes any time special ™

Love and GLORY
by LINDSAY McKENNA

Morgan's Mercenaries have captured the hearts
of millions of readers. Now, in this special
3-in-1 volume, discover the bestselling series
that began it all!

Meet the Trayhern family—bound
by a tradition of honor...and
nearly ripped apart by the
tragic accusations that
shadow their lives and loves.

"When it comes to action and romance,
nobody does it better than Ms. McKenna."
—*Romantic Times Magazine*

On sale April 2000 at your favorite retail outlet.

Silhouette®
Where love comes alive™